DEATH RIDE

Marc held on for his life. His feet slapped and bounced against the pavement as the van gathered more speed and he tried to keep from losing his grip on the door handle. He could see the passenger inside the van; blood was streaking down the side of the guy's face from a gash above his left eye. He was fumbling with a high-powered rifle and trying to get it pointed at Marc without having the driver in his line of fire. The muzzle finally came up and Marc knew there was no place to hide.

A fireball appeared from the muzzle of the scoped rifle and Marc felt the concussion torrent as it slapped into him with violent intensity. There was no sound, only a hellish ringing in his ears. The only thing he could think was the peculiar theory that the victim never hears the shot that kills him. Marc saw nothing and felt nothing. And in that instant he knew the grim reaper of doom had harvested him at last.

Bantam Books by Bob Ham:

Overload #1: PERSONAL WAR
Overload #2: THE WRATH
Overload #3: HIGHWAY WARRIORS
Overload #4: TENNESSEE TERROR
Overload #5: ATLANTA BURN
Overload #6: NEBRASKA NIGHTMARE
Overload #7: ROLLING VENGEANCE
Overload #8: OZARK PAYBACK
Overload #9: HUNTSVILLE HORROR
Overload #10: MICHIGAN MADNESS
Overload #11: ALABAMA BLOODBATH

OVERLOAD
Book
11

ALABAMA
BLOODBATH

□ □ □

Bob Ham

™
FALCON

BANTAM BOOKS
NEW YORK • TORONTO • LONDON • SYDNEY • AUCKLAND

Any similarity to persons, living or dead, places, businesses, governments, governmental entities, organizations, or situations, in existence or having existed, is purely coincidental.

ALABAMA BLOODBATH
A Bantam Falcon Book / June 1991

ISBN 0-553-29036-3

Published simultaneously in the United States and Canada

PRINTED IN THE UNITED STATES OF AMERICA
RAD   0 9 8 7 6 5 4 3 2 1

This one's for my good friend, Jim Southall—engi-eer, fellow radio amateur, and computer wizard—who has given abundantly and unselfishly of his time and vast knowledge both with research and technological support for the trials and triumphs of Marc Lee and Carl Browne. Without him, this book would have remained hidden in the deep, dark abyss of a hard disk on the night the printer died an agonizing death. I am forever indebted and eternally grateful for friends like you.

Thanks guy, and all the best

An evil man *seeketh only rebellion: therefore a* *cruel messenger shall be sent against him.*

PROVERBS 17:11

I will come forth with cleansing fire and devour the *evil scourge that profits from the misery of others.* *Hear my message well. For the doers of evil there* *is no sanctuary this side of hell.*

MARC LEE

Chapter One

□ □ □

The smell of salt along the wharf on Mobile Bay hung heavy in the air, permeating it. Like a thick perfume, the constant odor of the ocean in L.A.—Lower Alabama— smothered everything. The combination of decaying ocean creatures, common along the coast, along with the salt, gave the air an unforgettable aroma. The smell of death. But it was the smell of old urine from the open door of the rest room outside the quaint office at Miles Shipping and Drydock Company that stung into Rick Baxter's nostrils. A mole needed a good nose, but not necessarily one this good. Baxter had a good nose, a damned good one, but right now, he found himself wishing he didn't.

The most important thing to him now was his ears . . . the ones on his head and the one taped right up the middle of his butt and attached to the tiny microphone pressed against the inside of his pants crotch. The micro-miniature FM body transmitter was tuned to 174.945 megahertz and digitally encrypted to prevent unauthorized reception, which could prove fatal if it happened at the wrong time. The effective range of the transmitter was a half mile and the signal quality was exceptional. The microphone was sensitive enough to detect the sound of a pencil falling on the floor across the room, yet the noise-canceling circuitry prevented interference from Baxter's own movements. Without the ears, should something go sour, Baxter knew he was one dead narc. Fish bait.

Being here was one thing. Dying here was another matter altogether, so Baxter chose his words carefully when he spoke. He was careful not to allow his eyes to wander too far from the person he spoke to. A telltale sign of a narc—the nose. Too nosy and too interested in what was going on around him. Many a novice in the profession had not lived to become a veteran because of simple, seemingly insignificant mistakes like that. The ones hardened criminals could catch with their street-honed instinct.

Baxter knew the ropes and he knew the rules for survival *down under*. In his profession, you learned those ropes and rules quickly and accurately or you didn't have to concern yourself with them because you were dead. Rick Baxter had made a personal pact with himself long ago. He would rather retire from Drug Enforcement Administration than die in it.

He propped his feet up on the empty chair beside him in the dingy little office. The office sat fifty feet off of the edge of the long dock that lined Mobile Bay on the Gulf of Mexico. Outside, the ocean water slapped rhythmically into the side of the dock, creating a melodic tune that ingrained itself into the subconscious mind. And sometimes it was irritating.

The furniture in the room was sparse, tattered remnants, collected over the years, that had been mistreated, abused, and neglected by the occupants. There were chairs, a dozen or more of them and most partially broken, a wooden table once used to clean fish on the dock, and a battered wooden desk that had somehow survived since the 1940s. The floor was cold concrete covered with a film of time-hardened filth. The walls were plaster, not drywall, but the real thing, complete with wire-mesh grids for support. They were void of paint except for what little had not peeled from the corrosive abuse of the salty ocean air over the years. There were countless holes in them, too, some that provided a clear view into adjoining rooms, others that exposed the rough-hewn pine two-by-fours used to frame the walls.

The room had three possible entries and four exits. There was a door that led directly to the dock out back to the east. A large multipane window, smothered with years of dirt, provided a view of the docks. Or at least it would have had it ever been cleaned. Another door connected with a large storage room to the south, where the stinking rest room was. And the third, on the west side, came through the front of the building bordering the street. The front door could be found only after a winding passage through a maze of drygoods stored in the space near the street.

Baxter watched with trained eyes and carved it all into the recesses of his mind for instant recall as Bubba Ray Miles assisted and supervised two shaggy-haired street thugs counting pills. With a metal scoop, they dipped them from a thirty-gallon garbage can lined with a thick, black plastic bag. Then they spread them out on a piece of Plexiglas on top of the old fish table and sorted them with a plastic twelve-inch ruler. When they had sorted them, they scraped each batch off the Plexiglas and into a zip-top plastic bag. Then they moved each bag with the precise number of pills they wanted into a corrugated box sitting precariously on a wooden stool beside the table.

Bubba Ray sipped on a long-neck beer, then chewed on the ever-present cigar stuck between his teeth. He had brown hair; what little there was of it licked from the sides of his bald head and met, barely, at the back. He kept his hair cropped at the top of his shirt collar. His pudgy cheeks were like road maps, streaked with broken blood vessels and scarred from untreated childhood acne. His brown eyes sat deep in his face and gave him the sinister appearance of a corpse. His left front tooth was chipped, the result of a wharf-side brawl with a drunken longshoreman years earlier. When he smiled, an event that only occurred when he was counting money or pills, he looked hideous, like some refugee from a dark, dismal swamp.

He was the DEA textbook example of a lowlife criminal, an appearance Bubba Ray owed to family heritage and years of practice. His father, his grandfather, and even his great-grandfather had been notorious Alabama moonshiners. For four generations, the Miles family had retained a hard-earned reputation for violence and absolute disrespect for the law and those who enforced it. "Them revenuers come snoopin' around here stickin' their nose into mah family's livelihood. They ain't good fer nothin' 'cept sightin' in a varmint rifle," his father used to say. Bubba Ray maintained this philosophy and carried on the family tradition.

Bubba Ray had grown up thinking the wrong side of the law was the right side. At twelve, he drove decoy cars for his father and grandfather. At fifteen, he ran "shine" seven days a week. And by the time he was sixteen, his father had lost a gun battle with revenuers and he found himself orphaned. But that didn't bother him, because he also inherited the family moonshine business. And by the time he was seventeen, he was making more money in a month than the president of the United States made in a year. He turned twenty-one on a road gang, doing his part to keep Alabama beautiful. He was out at twenty-three, and so was the moonshine.

That's when Bubba Ray changed his life and found a better way to make a living.

Drugs.

Gone were the days of sitting day and night, day in and day out, by the moonshine still back in the hills. No longer did he have to endure rain, snow, or winter ice storms to scrape out a living. There was no more lugging sacks of sugar or barrels of corn into the backwoods. No more modified cars with hundred-gallon shine tanks. No more

Mason jars or plastic jugs stacked high in the woods near the mash barrels or ricks of hardwood drying in a row so the fire beneath the cooker would burn at just the right temperature. No. All of that was gone. Copper worms and copper cookers that would trickle out a crystal-clear brew that burned the prettiest blue flame known to man when subjected to a lit match . . . gone. In their place there were bricks, nickel bags, ten-cent pieces, boulders, uppers, and downers. Best of all, there were ludes. Big eighteen-wheel trucks loaded with methaqualone . . . Quaaludes.

Although it was after midnight, it was still business as usual at Bubba Ray's waterfront office. Tonight would mark the thirteenth buy in less than three weeks. It would also be the last. The long-awaited major shipment had arrived earlier in the night by truck from somewhere up north. Baxter suspected Detroit, Michigan. He was convinced of it, but he didn't have enough evidence to prove it in a court of law. When the packages were finished and the dealers came in off the street to get the next day's supply, hell was gonna break loose. Hopefully, it would break loose long before the goods could enter Bubba Ray's pipeline of eighteen-wheelers and be dispersed to his retailers around the country. The ear in the crotch heard everything, it had for several weeks now, and it sent it all to the Ampex multitrack tape recorder in the DEA van a block away on the street to the west.

The headphone-bearing snoops in the van weren't alone tonight either. There were six Mobile PD vice officers armed for war and itching to storm the dumpy little office and kick butt. With them was a crack team of six federal agents affectionately, although quite unofficially, called SCAT. That stood for Strategic Criminal Assault Team, and they were the best of the federal government's hard hitters. The SCAT guys, not unlike vampires, thrived on blood . . . criminal blood. They were scrupulously trained, exceptionally disciplined, and unerringly efficient. They were also an undercover narc's best friend, or his worst nightmare, depending on how the bust went down. And before the glittering rays of the morning sun streaked across Mobile Bay, Baxter knew he would find out which these guys were . . . best friends or worst nightmare.

Then there was a knock at the door and Rick Baxter felt his heartbeat skyrocket.

Party time.

Buddy Nichols lifted one headphone off his ear and turned to Mobile PD Lieutenant Charlie Drake who sat hard-faced in a lounge chair across from the electronics console. He turned back around and keyed the transmitter as he spoke into the microphone. "Okay, guys, we have an entrant. Get the teams into final checks and make ready. We could have a curtain call any minute."

"Just the one guy?" Drake asked. He watched the video monitor as it scanned and recorded the front of the drydock office facing the street.

"Yeah, that's all I saw," Nichols said. "We still don't have an accurate head count on the inside. That makes me nervous as hell."

"Not to worry, Buddy," Drake said. "If Miles suspected anything, he'd be out of that place like a scared jackrabbit. Baxter's cool. We'll take this thing down like clockwork. When it's a done deal, Bubba Ray Miles will be on a very, very long vacation and his dope kingdom'll tumble into the depths of the bay. At least whatever's left after the auction."

"Yeah," Nichols said. He pressed the talk switch on the console and made a general call to the officers stationed discreetly in and around the drydock. "Control to all units. Stand by, we have movement on the inside. Remember, don't let those boats get away from the dock and keep the eighteen-wheelers at the loading ramps. We want this quick and we want it clean. Do a final check of your hardware and get ready for the call."

"I'd like to stall this thing so we can get a full ID on as many local dealers as we can. The more of them Baxter can take down, the better," Drake said. He put on a headset so he could hear the transmissions that came by way of Baxter's concealed transmitter. He glanced at Nichols. "Is the dealer inside yet?"

"No, not yet. I hear a lot of movement inside. They must be playin' real careful in there," Nichols said.

Drake shook his head. "If you were dealing a million or more ludes a month, wouldn't you play it close to the chest, too? This guy must have nerves of titanium."

Nichols listened to the sounds coming over the transmitter. "Yeah, or he just doesn't care anymore."

The radio console crackled. "Control, SCAT one. We've got heavy movement near the boats. They're loadin' large plastic bags and wooden crates. I don't think it's long until they shove off. Give me an action code."

Nichols pressed the transmitter switch. "Ten-four, SCAT one. Stand by. We don't want to spook these clowns. You got the boat ID?"

"Ten-four, control."

"Okay, we can't jeopardize our man on the inside. He calls the shots. If the boat leaves, we'll have to rely on the Coast Guard to take him down before he hits open water. Keep him under surveillance and keep us informed."

"Ten-four. SCAT one clear."

Nichols decided to run a fast status check. "SCAT two, control. You set on the south dock?"

"Ten-four, control. Give the word and we're in."

"SCAT three, control. Front's still hot. You got it covered?"

"Ten-four, control. SCAT three is ready on your command."

Nichols charted the locations on a plastic overlay of the drydock and office building. "Okay, vice units one through six. Acknowledge in sequence."

The speaker crackled on the van's console. "Vice one, ready."

"Two in position."

"Three waitin' for the word."

"Four set."

"Five ready to kick butt."

"Six, we're ready."

Nichols assessed the situation. He pressed the talk switch once more. "Okay, guys, hang tight."

Drake smiled. "Now all we need is the code word from Baxter and we can take this hellhole down and it's a wrap."

"I've worked with Baxter before," Nichols said. "He'll wait until the last possible second to give the word. He likes to give his victims all the rope he can so they can tie the knots real tight. The guy is damned good at what he does."

"Must be," Drake replied. "He's still alive. I think what makes me so nervous is the fact that we've been after Bubba Ray Miles for six years. We've been able to get close, but we've never been able to pull his plug."

Nichols laughed. "Well, Drake, his plug is going to be pulled and his empire short-circuited before this night is over. I promise you that. You've never seen smooth until you've seen a SCAT unit close down an operation. They make Swiss precision seem archaic. These guys are the best I've ever seen. Bar none."

"I hope you're right. Every time we've tried to squeeze Miles, he's slipped through our fingers like a greased pig. I wonder if maybe the guy has a sixth sense of some kind that warns him when the doors of doom are about to slam shut on his backside. It's been incredible," Drake said.

"His luck's run out tonight. Bet on it," Nichols said confidently. "This is the last day of operation for Bubba Ray Miles and his centralized synthetic death ring. Just as soon as Baxter says the magic word, hell's gonna swarm right up Mile's ass with a fury the devil himself couldn't duplicate."

Drake strained to hear what was coming across the transmitter taped to Baxter's body. He listened and then he pressed the transmit switch on the electronic console in front of him. "Here, we go, guys. We got an entry code. Stand by, showtime's coming."

The knock at the door had been executed with precision to ensure the proper code. Anyone who didn't know that code stood an excellent chance of having a load of twelve-gauge double-ought buckshot answer the door.

"Check it out, Joe. Ahm sorta busy countin' these heah pills," Bubba Ray said in his best down-home drawl. He looked up and nodded his head toward Joe McNally, who sat across the room in a rickety chair unpacking cases of zip-top plastic bags.

McNally, who was just slightly smaller than the doorway and not quite as smart, dropped the carton he was working on and smiled at Miles. "Sure thing, Bubba Ray," he said. He moved without hesitation toward the door. When he got there, he leaned against the wall, wrapped his hand around the butt of a semiautomatic pistol, and yelled. "Yeah, whatta you want?"

Ronnie Richardson covered McNally from across the room. He held a twelve-gauge Remington 870 shotgun in his hands, aimed at the center of the doorway. The rear of the shotgun had a Choate synthetic pistol grip field stock. The fore end had been modified, and rather than the usual round horizontal handgrip, it, too, had a vertical pistol grip. Awkward, but effective. The barrel had been cut illegally to fourteen inches for close-range work. Its chamber held a round of ten-pellet double-ought buckshot and the magazine was alternately loaded with hollow-point slugs and more double-ought. Beside him in the corner was an Ingram MAC-10 .45-caliber submachine gun with butt-to-butt thirty-two-round magazines capped off to the maximum with Federal Hydra-Shok 230-grain hollow points. Deadly efficiency.

Rick Baxter tried to relax before the reply came from outside the door. He knew it was time for the dealers to start their merchandizing runs, and that made him nervous. It always had since the first day he got into the business. He had been in Mobile less than two months now and no one knew who he *really* was. That made recognition unlikely, but he had learned another lesson long ago. In the narc business, anything was possible. And recognition by an old acquaintance was absolutely a veteran narc's most dreaded possibility. It was also one of the deadliest.

There was no reply at the door.

McNally bellowed again, his voice more animal than human. "You stupid or what? I asked you who is it?"

Then a voice penetrated the heavy metal door. The person speaking was yelling, but his words came into the room just slightly louder than a whisper. "It's Castleman. Open the damned door."

"Oh," McNally mumbled. He worked the locks on the door and twisted the knob. When he opened it, he stood looking down at a man.

"Jeez, Bubba Ray," Castleman said without acknowledging McNally. "You got to get more modern around here. You need an intercom or a camera or something. You can't hear shit through that door when you're standing out there in that big ole room full of shit. Can't be good for business."

Bubba Ray kept counting pills until he was finished with the pile on the Plexiglas plate. Then he looked up and grinned at Castleman, who had stepped inside without waiting for an invitation. "How the hell are you, Jody? I trust you brought old Bubba Ray a big fistful of greenbacks, didn't you?"

"Don't I always? Why the hell else would I lower myself to come into a dump like this? I'm a businessman, Bubba Ray. I got an air-conditioned office, two secretaries, a fax machine, three computers, a BMW, and carpet so thick on my floor you'd think you're walking in snow. You could live better than this, Bubba," Castleman said.

"I live all right, Jody," Bubba said, and kept the grin going. "This here's just mah workin' place. Don't make me no difference how it looks. Ah been in places a damn site worse than this. Now, we was talkin' some business. How much can I do you for?"

Castleman's nose wrinkled when he took a long sniff of the air. "What's that smell, Bubba? It smells like week-old piss."

McNally laughed. "Smells like it 'cause it is," he said. "Damn john's been broke for a month or more. Never can remember to get the part to fix the mother."

Castleman shook his head in disgust. "Well, let's get this done and I'll be on my way. Hit me three thousand times. Ludes are hot in Mobile tonight, baby." He reached into his pocket and came out with a roll of money the size of a baseball. He removed a heavy rubber band from the roll and started counting out hundred-dollar bills. "Price still the same, Bubba? A buck a hit?"

"No inflation at Bubba's. Price is still the same." Bubba reached into the corrugated box and started counting out thirty plastic bags, each containing a hundred Quaaludes. He stacked them on the fish table beside the Plexiglas plate. When he was finished, he looked up at Jody Castleman and his face split wide with a smile. "It's a done deal. Thirty little bags all in a row."

"Good," Castleman said. He picked up the bags and put them in a plastic trash bag he had removed from his hip pocket. "I'd best be getting on my way."

Bubba lifted the bills from the table and counted them. He hit thirty, folded the money, and stuffed it into his shirt pocket. Then he looked at Castleman again. "It's a pleasure doin' business with you, Jody. Sell that batch and come on back in here for another load. We'll have 'em fresh and clean all the time."

"Yeah, Bubba, I'll be back in a few days. You can count on it," Castleman said. He lifted the plastic sack and headed for the door.

McNally opened the door, let Castleman out, and then locked the multitude of locks again. "Somethin' 'bout that man just don't sit right with me, Bubba," McNally said.

Bubba paid no attention to him, but went immediately back to counting out Quaaludes.

Minutes passed and then there was another knock at the door. McNally repeated the ritual of leaning against the wall and yelling, "Yeah, whatta you want?"

"Joe, it's Herschel. Open the damned door," the voice said from the other side.

McNally worked the locks and opened the door. Herschel Pope stood there. With him was another man, who appeared unusually nervous.

Pope came inside, followed by his friend. "Bubba, this is Billy Dwayne Filbert. He's one of my runners down toward I-ten. Billy just got in off a vacation with Uncle Sam. Did three years of a ten-year rap. He's cool and I asked him to help me move the goods tonight. Ain't no problem, is it?"

Rick Baxter tried to turn away as inconspicuously as he could. He recognized the face even before he heard the name. And it all crashed down on him like a raging bull. Billy Dwayne Filbert. Memphis, Tennessee. Three and a half years ago. He had busted the guy, held him on the floor with his pistol stuck against his nose after a serious struggle, and almost dropped the hammer on him.

Baxter played it cool, but inside, his stomach was churning. After all, back then there had been no beard and his hair was much shorter. But his face was still the same and there wasn't much he could do about that. Baxter held his breath and hoped the long hair and beard would disguise him adequately. He hoped, prayed, the druggie wouldn't recognize him.

Filbert looked around the room nervously. His eyes settled on Baxter and bored through him. He stared for a moment before he spoke. "Hey, dude, don't I know you from somewhere?"

Chapter Two

Nichols's voice was extremely excited as it crackled across the airwaves and came through the tactical headsets of the officers waiting to strike the drydock facade. "All units. Move to threshold and stage. We may have a sighting. Repeat, move to threshold and stage. We may have a sighting. Stand by for a hard takedown."

"Who's that guy with Pope?" Drake asked as he watched an instant replay of the video footage showing the two men entering the front of Bubba Ray's distribution depot.

"Beats me," Nichols said. "I've never seen the character before tonight. Maybe the computer will turn something on the name in a minute."

"A minute may be too late for Baxter," Drake said. "We got all those trucks at the dock and the boats waiting to speed across the bay and out into the Gulf. We can't let this turkey slip away again. There's probably more than a million hits of Quaalude and other crap inside those transportation devices. I want them and I want Mile's ass."

"Patience," Nichols said. "Don't get too excited until we see what's going to go down inside there. It may be a false alert."

"Patience, my ass," Drake said. "Mobile has had twenty-seven fatal accidents in the first six months of this year involving truckers on drugs. My bet says three-fourths of 'em bought the stuff from one of Miles's street thugs. The murder rate has jumped through the ceiling. Burglaries are up. Robberies skyrocketed. Thefts, rapes, hit-and-run fatalities . . . you name it, it's up. Want to know why? I'll tell you why. Drugs. There's a mainline into this city with tentacles that reach all over the South. Any pharmaceutical company would be proud to move as many drugs as these street thugs do. I got a mayor and a city council on my ass and a governor who wants to know why we can't curb the flow of illegal drugs into this city. They know and I know it's mostly the business enterprise of Bubba Ray Miles. Nobody's been able to prove anything or tie Miles into the network sufficiently to prosecute him until now. They want his balls and I want his ass."

"I can relate to that and I respect your feelings," Nichols said. His voice was calmer now, but he knew the adrenaline was still pumping because he could feel himself sweating. He tried to separate his personal feelings from his professional responsibilities, and at the moment, it wasn't very easy. "You must remember one thing. That's a damned good federal agent in there risking his life. He's not just any federal agent, he's my friend and I'm responsible for him. As long as I sit at this control panel and call the shots on this operation, I'm not going to make one move or permit anyone else to make one that could jeopardize his safety. Miles or no Miles. I want my man out of there alive. Bottom line. Nothing else matters. If we take Miles and his thugs, all the better. But if this thing turns, my man comes first. Is that clear?"

"I understand that, Nichols," Drake said. "I didn't mean to devalue Baxter, his job, or his life. You and me, it's our nuts on the line here. We can pull this off with no mistakes, get your man out, and put Bubba Ray's sorry rump in a sling in the process. That's all I want."

The computer printer started running with a clanking

chatter. Nichols stared at the printout as it cleared the carriage and dropped out the back side. When it stopped, he reached over and ripped the printed sheet free. He moved it under the small lamp used to illuminate the console. As he read it, his blood pressure shot upward. The heat flashes he had felt earlier were now full-fledged tremors.

Drake detected a problem. "What is it?"

"We may have a problem," Nichols said. "We got an ID on the name. Billy Dwayne Filbert has a criminal record a half mile long. He just got out of a federal corrections institute on a drug-related charge. They're running him now to see if Baxter was involved in the case. Follow-up should come over the link any second. If it's a hit, Baxter could be in over his head."

Baxter chuckled and stared Filbert directly in the eyes. He hoped it worked, because he knew what would happen if it didn't. He decided to play it cool and simple. "You must have me confused with somebody else, sport. I don't recall seeing you before."

Bubba Ray laughed. "That there's Denny Thompson. He's got hisself a little operation goin' over at the 'Bama–Florida line in them rich condos along the Gulf. Maybe you boys crossed paths somewhere."

"Not that I recall," Baxter reiterated.

Filbert let it drop, although he still appeared quite nervous, and Baxter breathed a sigh of relief. He stayed cool on the outside, but inside, he hoped he didn't piss in his pants and screw up the transmitter. He knew it was his only lifeline to the outside world. His only chance, albeit slim at best, to leave the grungy little room alive if something went haywire.

"What's for you tonight, Pope?" Bubba asked. He tried to get the conversation back to business. There wasn't time for guessing games when major money was to be made.

"Five thou, Bubba. What about free goods?"

"Two hundred with a five-thou order. Deal?"

"Deal," Pope replied, smiling. The percentage wasn't the best, but the availability was outstanding. And the day hadn't come when he would refuse two hundred free dollars.

"You still workin' them truckers, Pope?" Bubba asked.

"Just like clockwork. Got me a regular pipeline, Bubba," Pope replied.

Bubba counted fifty-two bags and placed them on the table. Pope opened a black nylon tote bag and placed all of the bags inside it. He zipped it closed and left it on the table. Then he counted out five thousand dollars in cash and dropped it on the Plexiglas plate beside the bag. "That ought to take care of things, Bubba. We'll see you after the weekend and do some more business."

"Please do," Bubba said, smiling. He folded the money and stuffed it into his shirt pocket with the first roll.

Pope picked up his bag and left the dingy office. Filbert followed after shooting one more menacing glance at Baxter.

Baxter breathed a silent relieved sigh when Pope and Filbert were on the other side of the closed metal door. Close calls did not arouse comforting feelings in his business.

Pope and Filbert were thirty feet through the outer room headed toward the street when Filbert stopped abruptly. He grabbed Pope by the arm and stared into his eyes. "Wait a minute, now I know where I know that guy from."

"Who?" Pope asked, but he kept walking.

"That guy callin' hisself Thompson. Well, it ain't Thompson, it's Baxter. He's a DEA narc, man. That son of a bitch is a cop!"

"Shit, Dwayne, are you sure?" Pope asked. He stopped abruptly. He looked at Filbert as if he didn't want to believe him, but his gut was telling him to man the battle stations because Filbert was right.

"Damn straight, I'm sure," Filbert said. His lips were quivering. I told myself I'd never forget that face. He didn't have a beard then, but I know it's that same guy. Mother almost shot me in the face three and a half years ago in Memphis. His hair was shorter then, too."

Pope grew instantly nervous. He stood there, silent and unmoving for several seconds. "We got to get out of here and find a way to let Bubba Ray know about this. He can handle it on his own," Pope said.

"Handle it, shit. I'm goin' back in there and waste that mother. He's the reason I done all that time. I want me some ass, Pope. Some narc ass." Filbert was angry now and that made him forget how nervous he was.

"Man, we can't go bustin' back in there accusin' that son of a bitch unless you're positive. If you're wrong and this cat is cool, Bubba Ray will kick our asses halfway across the bay and then feed what's left of 'em to the sharks."

"I'm tellin' you, dude, ain't no doubt in my mind. That's the cocksucker that sent me to the joint. I want his ass and I want it now," Filbert said. He could feel his blood pressure rising and he knew emotions were taking control of his sanity.

Pope hesitated. "C'mon, man. Goin' back in there is heavy-duty stuff. You just don't go back inside a source when you've got a done deal. It ain't good business. First thing they gonna think is we're gonna hit 'em. They got machine guns in there. We don't have any with us. I don't like it. Let's take our dope and get away from here."

Filbert was adamant. He shook his hand toward the office door. "You better like it. That federal narc just saw you make a major drug purchase. He saw me, too. That means more time in the joint when the bust goes down. They probably even got the place videotaped. They got us, man. You brought me straight out of the joint into the arms of a fed so's they can send me right back inside. I ain't goin', man. No way. I ain't goin' back to no joint for somebody else's dope. Hell no. We got to go waste that creep, Pope, and get rid of any evidence he might have stashed someplace. Ain't no other way, man."

Pope was still hesitant. He walked around in a tight circle for a long moment. Then he leaned against a bundle of drygoods stacked to the ceiling and looked Filbert directly in the eyes. "Okay, we go back in, but I do the talking until I tell you to speak. Bubba Ray ain't gonna be a real happy man. If they come down on us with those auto guns, you keep your cool. You mess up and Richardson will send hot lead through both of us faster than a runaway buzz saw."

Pope and Filbert walked back to the steel door that separated Bubba Ray's office from the outer storage room. Pope gave the coded knock and waited for McNally to growl on the other side. When he did, Pope responded. "It's Pope again. We forgot something."

McNally opened the door. Pope and Filbert found themselves facing the barrel of Richardson's sawed-off shotgun. They froze.

Bubba Ray looked up from the fish table and shot a hard look at Pope. "What is it, Pope? It ain't good business to come back after you made a buy," he said coldly.

Pope glanced at Baxter and then stared at Bubba Ray. "Bubba, my friend here says this man calling hisself Thompson ain't who he says he is. He says he's a federal narc named Baxter."

Baxter cringed, but kept his cool. He stood from his chair and moved slowly toward the fish table. He looked at Bubba Ray and then at Filbert. His eyes caught a glimpse of McNally across the room and Richardson poised with the Remington shotgun ready to breathe twelve-gauge death. Finally, his eyes settled back on Bubba Ray. "Boys, I been called a lot of things in my day, but never a narc. You better have something up your sleeve that I don't know about before you start callin' me a narc," he said, spitting fire from his eyes.

Bubba Ray's face was flushed red. He stared into Pope's eyes and his lips tightened. "Damn you, Pope. You've ruined mah pardy."

"What?" Pope said.

"I know who Baxter is. Always have. The joke's on him." Bubba Ray snapped his fingers and the room was instantly a den of chaos. Gun-toting, dock-hardened long-shoremen came through every entrance from every direction.

Rick Baxter held his breath when the cold steel muzzle of a pistol pressed against his temple. He knew this was the big one. It might also be the last one if he didn't talk very fast and very, very convincingly.

Nichols was screaming into the microphone. "All units! Move now! It's a hard takedown. They've made Baxter. Take the place down now!"

Almost immediately, the penetrating sound of contin-uous gunfire cracked the silence of the night and masked the rhythm of the waves slapping into the drydocks. The docks were a hellground of gunfire. Automatic weapons fired over and over, then the sound of a powerful boat engine revving roared over the gunfire. The boat sped into Mobile Bay and headed for the open water. But a whoosh streaked across the night sky and left a trail of burning propellant as a rocket from a DEA tube sought and found the power boat. A thunderous explosion roared and fiery debris rained into the sky then fell back into the ocean waters with sizzling impact.

Drake's hand wrapped around the pistol grip of a riot shotgun. He was out of his seat and heading for the door almost before Nichols finished the radio transmission. He opened the door and found himself looking into the shovel of a giant front-end loader that had materialized from the darkness. He fired a wasted shot of double-ought buckshot into the heavy steel shovel just an instant before the huge scoop slipped beneath the van and lifted it several feet into the air. Drake screamed and scrambled for the front of the van and another door.

Nichols lost his balance. The thrust of the van shifting on the scoop slammed him into the wall behind him. He hit with a brutal impact that dazed him for a moment. When he tried to regain his balance and senses, a mountain of electronic equipment came down on top of him from the console and pinned him against the van's wall.

The front-end loader bounced across the pavement until it reached the dock while Drake struggled to get the door open on the driver's side. He managed to shove it upward and open. He found a solid footing against the steering wheel and tried to get through the door. When he was almost free, he felt the van falling. He hit the cool ocean water first, followed a microinstant later by the van on top of him. Before he could fully realize what had happened, he sank into the depths of Mobile Bay beneath three thousand pounds of high-tech surveillance van and equipment.

Inside the dingy office, there was total chaos. At the first sound of gunfire, McNally had switched off the lights. People scrambled everywhere.

Rick Baxter hit the guy who held the gun at his head and knocked the weapon free. He spun to his right, knocking bodies out of his way in the darkness. Then he made a mad flying jump for the spot where he thought the dirty window would be.

It was there. He hit it broad-shouldered and crashed through. He felt the jagged edges of the dirty glass eat into his flesh as he crashed onto the dock outside. He landed on his side in a roll and spun around to get to his feet. In the process, his bloody right hand went beneath his jacket and came out with a Sig 9mm automatic pistol. Baxter took three or four steps toward the safety of a large stack of cartons on the dock, but then his chest was a blazing inferno that burned worse than anything he had ever known. A full load of double-ought buckshot tore through his flesh and devoured everything inside. He lost his balance and the pain was screaming from every nerve ending in his body and slamming into his brain at the speed of light. He fell to the dock against his will and lost his grip on the Sig. Then in the darkness, he realized he wasn't burning anymore. He was cold. Much colder than he should have been. But there wasn't any more pain, no feeling at all. Anywhere. His chest rocked, palpitated, and tried to get air, but there was none. For some unknown reason, it didn't matter anyway. When his eyes closed against a crashing sea of strange darkness streaked with arcing lights, there was nothing except peaceful silence.

All three SCAT units, each from a different direction, hit the office at almost the same time. Blazing hellfire scorched through the dark night as their automatic weapons fire sent death rounds in every direction. They made entry into Miles's office and found darkness there. Once they cleared the doors, more gunfire rattled and shook the walls.

The Mobile PD vice units hit the dock and surrounded the building. When they encountered little resistance, they moved on the office.

Then the darkness erupted into hellfire laced with sizzling death. Gunfire came from everywhere now. Shooters materialized from behind crates, out of darkened doorways, and from a line of eighteen-wheelers parked on the dock.

The SCAT units reacted first. They moved from the empty office and found themselves facing a wall of hot death hornets that streaked through the night. They retreated, tried to get into the office, but there was no cover of sufficient substance. Shooters were everywhere and death came from all directions at the same time. They fell back further along the dock, but another wall of hellfire confronted them.

The vice units were caught in the death trap before they could react. Miles's shooters came at them with lethal ferocity. Two vice officers were trapped behind a stack of fiber bales in the front room. They fired hard, selecting their targets, conserving ammunition. Then a dozen armed men moved toward them, gun barrels belching death and fire. When the officers tried to run for their lives, a barrage of streaming lead death swept them from their feet and sent them into eternity.

The SCAT units were fighting hard. SCAT one screamed for reinforcements over the tactical radio headset, but his call to the van went unanswered. The feds and vice units were outnumbered three to one as the fiery battle raged.

Both men of SCAT two found cover and engaged a half-dozen men from Miles's street-thug army in a heavy firefight. Two thugs caught death from SCAT weapons, but the other four charged with total disregard for their lives. When the SCAT units scrambled for a safe retreat, a hand grenade slammed into the concrete dock and exploded. Both SCAT men flew airborne in a sea of fire over the edge of the dock. Their bodies were ripped and torn before they hit the surface of the bay. Then they disappeared beneath the rolling water.

Bubba Ray Miles and two of his men had, at the first hint of trouble, moved through the side door leading into another dark warehouse section of the drydock building. They left Filbert and Pope to the mercy of the feds. Ronnie Richardson was the point man, leading Bubba Ray and McNally through the maze of crates and cartons stacked in the dark building. They took cover there and waited for the shooting to stop. It didn't, so Bubba Ray decided to escape without witnessing the end result of his "pardy."

"Ronnie, we can take the catwalk across the top of the building and get to them trucks parked at the end of the building. You go first and knock off any of them federal boys totin' guns out there," Bubba Ray whispered. "Mah boys can take care of anybody left nosin' around heah. I don't want a single one of them *po-leese* left standin'.'"

Richardson acknowledged and moved out. He climbed the ladder first and Bubba Ray followed. McNally took the rear and watched for trouble behind them. They reached the catwalk and moved across the top of the building until they neared the end. Then the gunfire came. A Mobile vice officer opened fire from behind an air-conditioning unit atop the roof. Richardson turned fast and dumped a barrage of death from the Ingram MAC-10. The cop fell over and the gunfire stopped, but the man was still alive on the roof top.

"Gimme that greasegun, Ronnie," Bubba Ray said.

"What are you gonna do, boss?" Richardson asked.

"I b'lieve that un's still kickin'. I'll be right back," Bubba Ray said. He moved from his protective prone position and went cautiously toward the fallen lawman. When he got there he could see the look of fear and pain etched across the guy's face, illuminated by the dock lights. "Howdy," he said as he kicked the guy's gun from his reach.

The wounded officer looked into Bubba Ray's face and glanced straight into the muzzle of the Ingram. "Miles, you're crazy. You can't kill cops and get away with it. They'll hang you for this. Somebody will find you."

Bubba Ray laughed and bit down on the stub of his cigar. "Hell, boy, I been hung like a mule since the day I was born," he said, and laughed louder. "As far as gettin' away with anythin', ain't nobody left alive that saw me. I never was heah. You boys ought to learn to mind your own business and leave us workin' folks alone. I'm gonna kill you now."

The cop's face tightened and his eyes pleaded for

mercy as he clenched his teeth. Then the Ingram barked a death staccato of .45-caliber Hydra-Shoks and the cop's muscles went limp.

Bubba Ray looked up into the night sky at the full moon and smiled. Then he turned his attention back to the dead cop and chewed the end of his cigar. He spoke as if the man could still hear him. "I told you weren't nobody left alive that saw me heah. Nobody."

Chapter Three

Marc Lee, Delta Force warrior turned Highway Warrior, sat on the sandy rise near the edge of a mesquite grove and watched the first penetrating rays of morning sunlight slip across the eastern Texas sky. His horse was lashed to a twisted limb on one of the mesquite trees and resting from the fifteen-minute ride to the rise on what had once been his family's ranch. Home.

From the gentle hillside, he could see the bottomland where his father had built a home and where he, as a child, had learned the necessary values of life to make him a man of reason and prudence. He had learned about honesty and trust. Loyalty. Dignity. Perseverance. There, on that very Texas soil, he had learned about *life*, about integrity. Often, the lessons were hard-earned. Frequently, they were painful. But they were lessons taught to him by the man he loved, respected, and admired every day of his life since he could remember.

That was all gone now, cast to the winds by a scourge that ran rampant on the Texas soil until the cleansing fires of unrelenting justice scoured the land and freed it of the virulent criminal bacteria that had wreaked havoc and destroyed the Lee family.

And now Marcus Lee, Marc's father, lay comatose in a safe house in Dallas. How long had it been? How long would it be? The man who had always been a giant in Marc's eyes lay in a deep sleep induced by the savages of mankind who lived for greed and perpetrated their madness upon innocent, decent people. And it had been that act of barbarian brutality that had started the never-ending war that now consumed Marc's life and that of his friend and partner, Carl Browne.

Their war against crime had at first been a personal one, but the record of their deeds had not gone unnoticed. And now they worked on a top-secret project, reporting to the president of the United States in a sanctioned assault on crime whenever and wherever they could find it. And find it they had. It was never far away . . . never far enough away. The war had raged in the corners of the country and in the heartland. In the cities, on the highways, and on the farms. The doers of evil knew no boundaries, respected no rights. But now the war was on their turf. And the rule book, battered against the will of the people and diminished to virtual insignificance by money-hungry or politically ambitious lawyers, had been cast aside like the true and equitable justice they had trampled into oblivion. The rules now were quite simple. Hit hard. Hit fast. Hit last. Do whatever must be done to rid the land of the criminal scourge that sucks the very lifeblood from the nation. More importantly, *win,* and live to challenge the criminal beast wherever his lair might be.

So now, in the midst of the war on crime that knew no end, Marc Lee and Carl Browne found days like the one now dawning to be further and further apart. Time for rest and relaxation had diminished in immense proportion to the rampage of the criminal element they sought to eradicate. Old wounds never healed completely and new ones waited behind the next closed door, but still the war raged on.

Marc looked down on the high-tech Leeco Freight Lines overroad eighteen-wheeler parked near where his family's house once sat. Beside it sat a horse trailer with steeds brought there by a family friend for Marc and Carl to enjoy while they took a brief respite from their chosen vocation. Inside the rig, Carl Browne was still sleeping in his bunk in the living quarters of the highly customized trailer. Jill Lanier, Marc's companion since childhood and now also a participant in the cleansing war, was asleep in Marc's bunk. Marc had grown restless in his sleep, awakened early, and decided to take an early-morning ride like he had done so many times as a young man. As he gazed down on the spot where his life had literally flown apart, the speaker crackled on the ever-present Icom U-16 hand-held radio clipped to his belt. Jill's voice broke the peaceful morning silence and his train of thought.

"Marc, Brittin is calling on the ComSat-D link. Hate to disturb you, but he says it's urgent." Jill's voice sounded sleepy.

Marc sat for a long moment before he answered.

Jill called again. "Come on, guy, I know you're out there. Answer me."

Marc lifted the transceiver and spoke. "Tell him I'll be back in fifteen minutes or so. It can wait."

"Okay," Jill replied. "I'll fix some coffee and have it ready when you get back. You're up on the hill, aren't you?"

"Yeah," he replied instinctively, still lost in memories.

"Okay, I thought you were. Enjoy it. From the sound of Brittin's voice, this little vacation isn't going to last much longer."

"I never thought it would," Marc said. He clipped the radio back on his belt and relaxed while the glow of the sun rising in a ball of fire crept over the eastern horizon. He watched it for several minutes, then climbed on his horse and rode hard toward the Leeco rig.

Jill had coffee steaming and the aroma filled the living quarters of the rig's trailer when Marc walked in. "Eighteen minutes. You're losing your timing."

Marc smiled. "I had to take in just a few more minutes of sunrise. I miss those."

Jill returned the smile. "I suppose that's just another casualty of this war. Will it ever end, Marc?"

"It may, but I'm not so sure any of us will be around to see it," Marc replied. "Where's Carl?"

"In the shower." Jill handed Marc a cup of coffee.

"Thanks," he said. "What else did Brittin say besides call him quickly?"

"He just said he needed to talk with you as soon as possible. Like I said, he sounded excited."

"Wonderful," Marc said, and he sipped the coffee. He sat at the electronics control console and stared at the Shure microphone. "Where is he—so I'll know which link to use?"

"He's at the Bureau in Washington," Jill said.

Carl emerged from the shower wearing only clean jeans, and he dried his hair with a towel. "Mornin', bro. You called him yet?"

"Nope. Get yourself a cup and sit in on the conversation. If he's got something going, I don't want you to miss any of it."

Carl pulled on his shirt and got a cup of coffee. He slid a chair from beneath the console table and sat down beside Marc.

Marc pressed the talk switch. "Barnburner, this is Pathfinder on Delta uplink. Over."

Seconds passed. Then Brittin Crain's voice crackled from the radio speaker. "Pathfinder, this is Barnburner. Thanks for returning the shout, Colonel. I apologize for getting you up before breakfast, but this one's sizzling hotter than a fried egg. Are you ready to copy? Over."

"Ready," Marc said. He sipped the coffee again, then sat it down on the console.

"Okay, Pathfinder. This one could get nasty. First, how long do you estimate it would take you to drive to Mobile?"

"Alabama?" Marc asked.

"Affirmative."

"Oh, ten, maybe twelve hours without pushing it too much. What's up?"

"To steal one of your lines, the defecation has engaged the rotary oscillator down there. This call came from the Boss himself. He's got a request from the governor of Alabama for federal assistance. The wheels of bureaucracy take time to turn, and the Boss says we don't have that long to wait. He says this mission is yours."

"It's always nice to be needed, but nicer to have a choice," Marc said.

"Oh, the choice is yours, too. You can take it or you can take it. Simple, really," Crain said.

"You're just jealous because we're in Dallas and you aren't. What's the scoop?"

"You're familiar with the USS *Alabama*, aren't you?"

"Affirmative," Marc replied.

"Good. I want you to meet me and Harvey Harrison on board the *Alabama* at nine o'clock tonight. We'll be in the captain's quarters. You should have plenty of travel time. If there are any problems, call on the link. I think all three of you should come," Crain said.

"Sounds interesting. What's up?" Marc asked.

"Fourteen dead cops and a weasel that knows enough magic to do a vanishing act. It's the worst bloodbath the law enforcement community of this country has ever known in the line of duty at any one time."

"So maybe you should call a magician on this one," Marc said.

"I just did. And from what we know now, you'll need every stroke of magic you can find in your bag of tricks. See you at nine."

Bubba Ray Miles sat on the sofa in the house at his luxurious farm forty miles north of Mobile. He chewed the tip of an imported cigar and made no attempt to conceal his aggravation. He looked at the investigator, Tommy Duncan, and for show, spat fire from his eyes. "Ah told you five times a'ready. Ah never left the farm night before last. Ah got me a dozen witnesses that'll testify in yo' court if it's necessary. If there was somethin' goin' on at mah drydock company, ah have no knowledge of it. Ahm sorry so many of your lawman brothers lost their lives, but ah know nothin' 'bout it. Ah heard it on the news just like everybody else. Now, if ahm a suspect, and ahm sure ah am, then you go ahead and charge me or get the hell out of mah house."

Duncan was unmoved. He stared at Miles and returned the fire from his eyes. "Miles, you're involved in this. You know it and I know it. I *will* charge you, sooner or later. Somewhere, you'll let something slip. You can play cat-and-mouse, but a lot of good, dedicated law enforcement officers are dead. They died on your property, trying to capture you and your drugs. You'll go down for this one. I can promise that."

"Sahgent Duncan, ah've been polite and me and my employees have bent over backward since the day before yesterday to assist your department on this heah investigation. Ahm damned tired of every time there's a killin' in these parts you boys come runnin' to me or somebody who works for me. Ah got the best lawyers money can buy and ah don't have to tolerate harassment from you or nobody else. Ah got mah rights, and right now you're violatin' the hell out of 'em. Do you want to quit heah or do ah call mah lawyer and file a harassment suit against you and your department?" Miles's voice was cold and deep. His eyes never left Duncan's. When he was finished, he relit his cigar and blew a puff of smoke skyward. Then he smiled.

Duncan stood and stared back at Miles. "Bubba Ray, somewhere, someday, you'll slip and fall. And when you do, someone who represents justice will be there to render a swift kick in your lard ass. We might start playin' by *your* rules. You know, *when a man's down, kick him*. You can count on it."

Bubba Ray's face tightened. He kept the penetrating stare spitting fire and never backed off. "Ahm lookin' fo'ward to you tryin', Sahgent Duncan. Better men than you already have . . . and they failed. So will you. Despite what you heathens think, there's nothin' there for you to find. Ahm just a Alabama country boy who done good and you can't accept that. Have a nice day."

Duncan turned and walked toward the doorway across the splendidly appointed room. He stopped, his hand on the gold-and-crystal doorknob, and looked back at Bubba Ray. He pointed his right index finger at him and held it firm. "Someday, Bubba Ray, your day of accountability will come. And payback is hell . . . in more ways than one. I guarantee it!" He reached into his pocket and switched off the tape recorder. There was enough there to satisfy anyone. A broad smile creased his face when he left Bubba Ray's house. Business was good.

The drive from Dallas to Mobile had been leisurely throughout the day. Carl drove most of the way, while Marc rode shotgun in the passenger seat. Jill relaxed in the sleeper of the comfortable cab and kept her head poked through the curtains to carry on a conversation while the miles clicked by with vanishing white lines.

When they reached Mobile, they drove over the bay on I-65 and checked out the area where the USS *Alabama* lay anchored. They decided to drive one of the Jeep Cherokees stored in the trailer rather than attempt to weave the rig through the maze that led to the parking area designated for tours of the old warship. They found a truckstop at I-10 just beyond I-65 and parked the Leeco rig there. Then they off-loaded the red Cherokee and secured the rig. Marc drove east until they reached the exit that would take them to the *Alabama*. When they finally made the parking lot, it was vacant except for two light-colored sedans. Marc glanced at his watch and saw it was 8:45.

"We're early, but I guess it won't matter," he said as he parked as close to the entrance to the warship-turned-tourist-attraction as he could get.

"I see the welcoming committee," Carl said as the Jeep's headlights fell upon two men in business suits who stood leisurely near the entrance ramp of the ship. "Two of the FBI's finest."

"I wonder why he wanted to meet here?" Jill asked.

"Security would be my guess," Marc replied. "How much safer can you get than a vacant ship docked in a bay. The tourists are long gone and they probably have the run of the place. Besides, I kind of like the idea. An old battlewagon sounds like as good a place as any to start a new battle, huh?"

Jill laughed. "Yeah," she said. "An old warship and a brand-new battle in another old war. Appropriate, I suppose."

Jill, Marc, and Carl left the Jeep and walked toward the ramp. The two men in business suits met them halfway. Before the Highway Warriors could speak, one of the men initiated a conversation.

"Colonel Lee, Major Browne, and Miss Lanier, I'm Special Agent Donald Crossfield and this is Special Agent Tim Barnes. Glad to see you here."

"Gentlemen, nice to meet you," Marc said.

"Same here," Carl replied.

"Yeah, me too," Jill said.

Crossfield shook hands with the warriors and then Barnes did the same. Crossfield turned and gestured toward the ship. "If you folks would be kind enough to follow me, Agents Harrison and Crain are waiting for you in the captain's quarters. The ship is empty except for us, so you needn't be concerned with security."

"She certainly is a stately-looking old tub," Carl said as they walked up the gangway.

"Yes, she is," Barnes said. "She saw a lot of hellfire in her time. She's a thirty-five-thousand long-ton battleship. Her prime was during World War II. When the navy decided to take her out of service and put her in mothballs in the early 1960s, the people of Mobile, all of Alabama in fact, raised money to restore her and make her what she is today. People come from all parts of the country just to stand on her decks and daydream about her days of glory."

"Nice guns," Marc said as he looked to her top deck at the rotating gun turrents. "How long have Crain and Harrison been here?"

"About an hour," Crossfield said. "After the boat closed for the day, we swept it and then they boarded. They have slides and some videotape footage for you. Strikes me as unusual, though. Why are military people like you guys called in on something like this?"

"Well," Marc said. "I'm not sure what *this* is. We're here following instructions. That's all I can tell you. When the Boss barks, we listen."

"Yeah, a lot of that going around," Crossfield quipped. He exited the top of the gangway and stepped onto the upper deck of the historic old battleship.

Marc, Carl, and Jill followed. Barnes brought up the rear and checked behind himself to be sure there was no one else in the parking lot or near the ship.

"This way," Crossfield said. He led the Warriors across the deck until they reached a small door near the tower. He opened it and stepped inside. A narrow and steep stairway led to the lower deck. Dim, but adequate lights glowed along the way. Movement was slow and footing uncertain as the entourage made their way belowdecks.

They reached the lower deck and moved along a narrow hallway through open watertight airlock doors until they reached the doorway marked Captain's Quarters.

Crossfield knocked on the door, then opened it, stepped inside, and gestured for the Warriors to follow him.

They did.

Two men sat across the small room. They reviewed files and maps. When the door opened, both of them looked up simultaneously.

Brittin Crain spoke first. "Hi, guys, it's been a while. Come on over and find yourselves a chair. I apologize for the accommodations, but under the circumstances, I felt this would be the place that would best suit our needs."

"Still findin' time for the weight room, I see," Marc said. "You look like a gorilla in a business suit, Brittin."

Crain laughed.

"Don't listen to him, Brittin," Jill said. "You still look great."

"Carl," Crain said, and extended his hand. "How goes it, brother?"

"Still hangin' in there, Brittin, but we all have our days," Carl said as he accepted Crain's hand.

Special-Agent-in-Charge Harvey Harrison exchanged greetings, then looked at Barnes and Crossfield. "Position at each end of the hallway. We don't want to be disturbed unless this tub is under attack or sinking. No one comes in. Period."

"Yes, sir," Crossfield said. "We'll take care of it."

Everyone sat down and then Brittin Crain opened a file folder. Inside was a photograph of a man in his late twenties or early thirties. Crain flipped it on the table where everyone could see it. "That's Special Agent Rick Baxter of the DEA. He died two nights ago right across the bay from where we're sitting now. He was murdered along with thirteen of his companions. They were shot down in cold blood during a planned raid on a major drug distribution location. From all appearances, the hit team for the bust was set up in a big way. Once they were inside, they were hit from the front and behind. A crack federal SCAT unit was completely mowed down. Seven dead feds and seven from Mobile PD vice. Two street thugs were gunned down. A man named Pope, Herschel James, and another named Filbert, Billy Dwayne. They were after this man, Miles, Bubba Ray, and that is his real name. He's the major-league source in these parts for all sorts of illegal substances. Former moonshiner and a permanent go-to-hell attitude. I have a complete file on him and several of his accomplices. To make a very long story very short, the Boss wants you to find Bubba Ray and end his kingpin empire. No one can prove he was involved, at least not yet, but we're spending hundreds of man-hours on his case as we speak. We can't prove it in a court of law, but it's proven to the satisfaction of the Boss. His instructions are to topple the kingdom and end the king's reign. In the process, find the leak inside of Mobile PD, the DEA, wherever it is, and plug it. Permanently."

No one spoke, but shocked, blank faces stared at each other.

Marc stared at the file and the photographs. "Bubba Ray seems to be a mean man. Is he as vicious as this would indicate or has he just built himself a reputation?"

"Oh, he's mean, all right. He'd kill his mother if he thought he could make a buck on the deal," Harrison said. He's a primo hardcase in the first degree."

"Is he smart enough to pull off something this incredible without getting caught?" Carl asked.

"Apparently," Crain said. "He's still a free man. There is nothing, repeat nothing, left of physical evidence that would place Miles at the scene of the murders. The guy is frightening. What he lacks in education, he makes up for in guts. He fears nothing."

"Get in on the inside," Harrison said. "Get on Bubba Ray's good-ole-boy roster, then pull his plug and bring his kingdom down. You'll have the support you need, but I must warn you . . . this man is a cold-blooded killer who does it because he likes it. All of his men are puppets. He pulls the strings and they dance. They'll cut your throats and feed your guts to the fishes if you mess up. It's a one-shot deal. Study the portfolios, the slides, and the videotape. Move at your leisure. Just one hitch."

"And that is?" Marc asked.

Harrison sat stone-faced. He glanced up from the folders and stared at the Warriors. "The Boss wants it wrapped up with ribbons on it within two weeks."

Chapter Four

□ □ □

"Ah don't care what it takes," Bubba Ray said as he looked into Reggie Stillman's eyes. They were in the extensively refurbished office of Miles Shipping and Drydock Company. "Ah got a hundred and twenty gallons of ludes that ah want on the street. Them damned things don't make me no money sittin' in a warehouse somewhere."

"Bubba Ray, we got the heat on big time. Everywhere we go, there's another surveillance unit watchin' somebody. I've never seen so many plainclothes cops on a case in my entire life. They ain't takin' it too well since we killed all their brothers the other night. We got to make every move real careful. One slip and they'll be on us like stink on shit."

"Ahm not gonna put up with it, Reggie. Them po-leese want a war, I'll give 'em a war. They ain't seen me mad yet. Ah just been teasin' 'em so far," Bubba Ray said. "Ah want ever' one of them eighteen-wheelers on the road and ah want all the stuff out of the warehouse and into the hands of our people. Hell, they're yellin' from Corpus Christi. Houston's runnin' low. Nawth Flawda ain't had a load in two weeks. Now, Reggie, we're in business to make money heah. Why let a little thing like a buncha narcs spoil our business?"

"It's a tall order, Bubba," Stillman said. "Some of our

boys is a little nervous since that shootin' thing the other night."

"Ain't no thing," Bubba said. "All we got to do is get innovative like we did back when we ran shine. Why, we had them federal boys layin' and waitin' 'round every other curve, but that didn't keep us from runnin' our shine. We had a market to deliver to and we made them damned deliveries. Ever' last one of 'em. Just got to think a little smarter than the next fella, that's all."

Stillman studied a computer printout from his stack of files. He was absorbed in heavy thought for several minutes, then he looked up at Bubba Ray. "We got twelve big trucks we can pull from service in Gulf Coast Cartage. We got almost enough drivers. I'd feel better if we had three or four more."

The sound of excited voices penetrated the office from the dock outside. Then a loud thud sounded when a man's body slammed into the wooden wall of the office.

"What's all that ruckus out there?" Bubba Ray asked. He clamped down on his cigar and walked toward the door.

"I'll check it out," Stillman said. He also stood and walked toward the door.

Neither of them got there before the door swung open and one of Bubba's dock workers staggered into the office. The man was tall, but slumped over. He weighed over two hundred pounds. His face was weathered from too many days in the Gulf Coast sun and too much salt-filled wind from the Gulf breeze. He draped his arms over Bubba's shoulder to maintain his balance and support his rubber legs as he stumbled. His rough face was bleeding profusely from a laceration on each side. Blood oozed from his shattered lips and there was a gaping hole where two teeth had been moments before.

Bubba Ray helped the man remain standing and slid the cigar from his mouth. "Tommy Dalton, what in the name of creation is goin' on out there?"

Dalton's words came hard between labored breathing. "Mr. Miles, they's two men out there on the dock and they're beatin' all hell outta everybody."

"What?" Bubba Ray asked. "Who are they?"

"Ain't never seen 'em before, Mr. Miles. They drove up in a big ole fancy eighteen-wheeler and said they wanted to talk to the man what run the place. Billy Joe told 'em you wasn't here. They said they wanted to talk to the main man and they wasn't goin' no place till they did. A coupla the boys tried to run 'em off and that's when the fightin' started," Dalton said with great difficulty. He stopped trying to speak and wiped blood from his face on his shirtsleeve. "It's some big white guy and a colored boy. You ain't never seen the likes of what's goin' on out there, Mr. Miles. I know I ain't."

"Hmm," Bubba Ray mumbled. He let go of Dalton's arms and stepped away. The big man crashed to the floor with a resounding thud and just lay there quivering. "Think I'll take me a look-see," Bubba Ray said, and moved to the door.

Stillman was right behind him. "Me too," he said.

Bubba Ray opened the door and stepped cautiously onto the dock. Just as his feet touched the concrete, the body of another dock worker slammed backward, stumbling. The guy collapsed at Bubba Ray's feet and remained motionless. Blood trickled from the side of his head and pooled onto the dock.

Bubba Ray couldn't believe what he saw. "What the . . ." he mumbled, but the words never cleared his throat before he ducked inside the open doorway to dodge another of his longshoremen sailing backward.

The battered man hit the dock, moaned, then went limp.

Bubba Ray stepped back on the dock and watched. There were ten of his men attacking the two guys, but the two truck drivers, if that's what they really were, kept his men at bay. Bubba Ray watched, stunned and amused.

A tall, beefy longshoreman slipped back from the attackers and fisted a four-foot section of iron pipe from beside a stack of crates. He held it beside his leg and weaved through the attackers toward the two guys from the eighteen-wheeler. He looked long and hard before he selected the black guy as the recipient of his rage. He lunged forward, the pipe now poised above his head and flying downward in a punishing arc as he made his attack.

Carl Browne saw it coming long before the guy lunged. He backstepped, ducked, and grabbed the pipe in the middle of the swing. He held it firmly, using the longshoreman's momentum for leverage. He flipped the pipe from the man's hands and twisted away. A sweeping swing with the weapon hit the longshoreman in the ribs. The guy screamed, choked, and gasped for breath. Then Carl sent the pipe sailing over the lip of the dock and into the water of Mobile Bay. His left foot came out in a flying snap kick and hit the longshoreman in the knee. The big man collapsed to the dock, landing on his other knee. A right-front snap kick caught his jaw and sent him reeling into unconsciousness on the surface of the dock.

Two more men moved forward while the others, stiff-faced and mean, taunted and encircled the Highway Warriors. One went for Carl and the other lunged for Marc.

Marc met the guy on his own turf. He lunged forward and challenged the onslaught. His right arm flew out to block a punch thrown by the longshoreman. He backpedaled and threw a kick with his left foot at the same time. He raked across the guy's legs and sent him crashing to the dock. A swift kick from his right foot caught the guy beneath the chin and sent him into darkness. When he looked up, another mean face moved toward him.

Carl blocked the second attacker's punch. He sidestepped, a left hook coming along with his momentum. His big fist landed squarely on the dock worker's face and sent him sideways. But the guy recovered and lunged for Carl. The Highway Warrior backpedaled, sidestepped, spun around, and sent a roundhouse kick into the longshoreman's ribs. The attacker buckled and fell to the dock surface gasping for breath.

Marc ducked when a sunburned man came at him with a barrage of right-left combinations. He swiveled right, then ducked again to his left. The man came with more ferocity now. Marc was up, his right fist flew forward and landed on the guy's jaw. Then he stepped back and out of the way of another right-left combination. The attacker was undaunted. He came on harder. Marc met him with a flying scissor kick that landed squarely on the longshoreman's chest and sent him reeling. When he hit the concrete of the dock, Marc was beside him. He lashed out with the heel of his boot and kicked the guy in the side of the head. The longshoreman rolled hard right and then spread out on the dock . . . unconscious.

Six of the longshoremen lunged for Marc and Carl at the same time. The Warriors broke immediately into their best karate-based defenses. Marc moved right while Carl broke away to the left. Both Highway Warriors tore into their assailants with the intensity of angry runaway buzz saws. Their hands and feet worked in unison with their brains and the result was a choreographed assault on the attackers unlike anything any of them had ever seen.

The last man fell seconds after the final assault started. Marc stepped over the fallen men and walked toward Bubba Ray Miles, who stood steadfast by the doorway and chewed excitedly on his cigar. He looked down at Miles and smiled. "You the main honcho around here?" he asked. His voice was even and determined.

Bubba Ray used his cunning and played cool. "Depends on who's askin'," he said.

"Name's Marc Lee and this here's my partner, Carl Browne," Marc replied.

Miles studied Marc and then he focused on Carl. The image registered in his mind of a dockful of his best men sprawled out on the cool concrete like so many fish fillets. "Well, boy, the name sure does fit yo' friend. Ahm Bubba Ray Miles. Somebody piss you off or what?"

"Naw," Marc said. He overplayed the Texas twang and down-home stupidity to such an extent he hoped it didn't come off as corny. "Me and Carl, here, well, we just come to have a talk with you. That's all."

Miles grew immediately suspicious and instantly defensive. "What in hell about? What can ah do fer you boys?"

Marc sensed Miles's uneasiness and smiled. Then he offered his hand. "We're truckers. Got our own rig, but times are a little slow. We come here to talk to you. Heard down at the truckstop on I-ten that you got the best operation runnin' in these parts. Then, of course, your tough guys got all twisted and tangled outta sorts about somethin'. Sorry 'bout that. Didn't mean no harm. We're lookin' for work."

Bubba Ray ignored the handshake offer but returned the smile as he slid the cigar from his teeth and held it between his stubby fingers. "Well, ah don't reckon ah have to ask too much 'bout yo' qualifications." He gestured with his hand at the injured longshoremen strewn around the dock like bags of litter tossed about by an angry junkyard dog. "That's purdy well obvious. Step into mah office where it's mo' private and let's us talk about some ref'nces."

The idea was a long shot at best and the inherent risk was substantial. But at the suggestion of Marc and after sufficient prodding by Brittin Crain, Jill Lanier decided to be a good sport and make a go of it. *One for the roses*. The instant she walked into the vice squad room at Mobile Police Department and saw the unconcealed suspicion burning in the eyes behind the desks, she wondered if perhaps she had been overly zealous. She rationalized, for the benefit of sanity and the strength to keep walking, that if she had been, it wouldn't be the first time and probably wouldn't be her last.

Damn you, Marc Lee. Screw you, Brittin Crain. She would have said the words aloud instead of just thinking them had it not been for the plastic smile she managed to stretch across her face. She strolled to the rear of the room and knocked on the door with small black letters painted across the scuffed wood surface: Captain X. Auxton.

"It's open," the voice growled from the other side.

She stood firm and erect. Poised. But inside her guts churned and her brain buzzed. *"X"? Who the hell would name their kid a name starting with an X? X Ray? No. Xylophone? Couldn't be. Xerox? Surely nobody would do that to a kid. Ah, Xavier. Yes, it had to be.* She put her hand on the knob, twisted, and pushed the door open in a steady, gentle motion. "Captain Auxton, I'm Sergeant Jennifer Lane."

A giant black man emerged from behind a desk that was more scuffed than the door it hid behind. He moved to the door, this giant, all six feet, eight inches of him. He had to weigh close to 260 pounds and his hands were mammoth. He reached the door beside her and closed it as gently as she had opened it. "I'm Zave Auxton," he said. "That's Zave, like Dave only with a Z." He offered his hand. "You're living proof the governor can work miracles with bureaucratic red tape when he wants to."

Jill accepted timidly and noted that the big man's index finger alone looked as large as her wrist. And that, considering the nature of the assignment, did not thrill her at all. "I'm pleased to meet you, Captain. Do we have time to talk?"

"My time is your time. That's what the chief says and the mayor says and the governor says. Of course I have time to talk. Please have a seat," he said, but the tone of his voice indicated obligation rather than willingness.

Auxton gestured with his mammoth hand toward a maroon leatherette chair awkwardly askew in front of his desk and Jill obliged.

"Could I get you some coffee? A soda maybe?"

"No, thanks," Jill said. *Soda? In the South?* "I try to stay away from caffeine as much as I possibly can," she replied. "Are you a native of Mobile, Captain Auxton?" The smile continued to stretch her face and her blue eyes danced a calypso rhythm as they scoured the room. Discreetly of course. So discreetly and imperceptibly that even a streethoned crime warrior like Auxton couldn't perceive it. It had to be that way because right now, everyone, including the big street cop who commanded the Mobile Vice Squad, was suspect.

"Too bad," Auxton said with a laugh. "Me, I live off of caffeine. Now, Sergeant, to answer your question, no, I am not a native of Mobile. Detroit, actually. And you?"

"Oklahoma City," Jill replied. She was amazed how quickly and easily the lie came. But, she reasoned, Oklahoma City was close enough to Dallas that she could fake it unless some pertinent question slipped through her mental filter and tripped her up.

"Oklahoma City is nice, or so I've heard. I've never been there myself. Out of curiosity, did my accent give me away? I thought I'd lost that long ago," Auxton said.

"Yes," Jill said, lying. "It was the accent. You don't sound Southern born and raised like so many of the locals. Maybe it's just my perception. These days, you can't tell reliably because people are so transient."

"Yes," Auxton said reluctantly. "I'd have to agree with that. Now, since we both know this isn't a social call to discuss family heritage, what can I do for you?"

"I know it's a rehash of what you've done a dozen times in the last few days, but I need to run through everything you know about the intended drug bust and eventual murders a few nights ago."

As Auxton slid back into his chair, worry and fatigue became evident across his face. "That's not an easy subject for me, Sergeant. Those men, every damned one of 'em, were my friends. I even trained some of them. They were good, dedicated men who believed in what they were doing. They had to, or they wouldn't have served the city of Mobile in this unit. They were gunned down like rabid dogs and this city is worse off for it. They were damned good men and they didn't deserve to die like that."

"I share your feelings, Captain. Do you, in your gut, believe Bubba Ray Miles was behind these killings?"

"Hell, believe it? I know it! Everybody from here to Montgomery knows it, too. The only problem we got is there's nothing, not one shred of evidence, to put Miles at the scene of the killings. Bottom line . . . we can't prove it in a court of law. And that is what this system of so-called justice requires, isn't it? Prove it in a court of law before a jury of the defendant's peers."

"I've read the reports and studied the information until I almost have it memorized, Captain. What is your opinion about that fatal night?"

"My scenario, from any angle it's viewed, comes to one simple conclusion. My men and the DEA were set up. Somebody, namely Miles, had their number and he planned to void their tickets that night. He did a damned efficient job of it, too. We've interviewed every redneck we can find who ever walked on Miles Drydock's shipping platform and we have turned up a big fat goose egg. Now you tell me, Sergeant, how do fourteen exceptional lawmen get their heads or their asses shot off and nobody knows a thing about it?"

"Who had knowledge of the raid or the surveillance that night?"

"The list is in my report. If you don't have a copy, I'll

see that you get one before you leave today. Every man who had knowledge has been questioned, interviewed, polygraphed—you name it and we've tried it. We haven't come up with squat."

"Could it have been one of your men on the drug enforcement team?"

"It could've been the damned mayor for all I know. If I knew who the son of a bitch was, I'd personally put a bullet right between his rotten eyes. That, Sergeant Lane, would be justice. As far as one of my men on the raid, no. Those guys were all friends. They worked together and played together. If they wanted to roll over and get dirty, they had more than enough opportunities without chancing something as heavy as murder-one haunting them the rest of their lives."

"What's your call on the screw-up?" Jill asked.

"Setup and leak. My gut says it had to be within the DEA. Not just because I run it, but I say Mobile Vice is squeaky clean. If I find out it wasn't, then there's liable to be another cop killin' before the thing ends. And I don't think anybody would shed too many tears for that one."

"All the DEA people were killed, too, Captain. That includes their man on the inside. And Baxter was, from all reports and evaluations, a textbook undercover officer. An experience-honed veteran who had done deals much tougher than this one and lived to testify about it. Do you think someone in a position of knowledge inside the DEA would burn their own kind?"

"Sergeant, when it comes to a network like the one Bubba Ray Miles operates, a network with eighteen-wheelers spreadin' out like spokes on a wheel to all points in the South, with his death dope and dealers, who buy from him and only him, on every street corner, I figure a guy who could pull the play would sell his own mother."

"So where would you suggest I start looking, Captain?"

"Let's don't play games with each other, Sergeant. You

and I both know you started looking the second you walked through my office door." Auxton let his cupped hands fall to the top of his desk. He leaned forward and stared a piercing smile into Jill's blue eyes.

Jill said nothing, but she focused her eyes on his and thought back to her upbringing in Texas. She knew she had read it somewhere and she knew it was true. *The eyes are the window to the soul*.

"If it'll ease your mind any, I'm not your man. But I'll tell you this, I'll do *anything* to help you or anyone else find the person or persons responsible for the death of my friends. And when I do, I can guarantee you it's not going to be a pretty sight. If I find him first, he's gonna know what hell's like a long time before he gets there."

Jill kept her eyes focused on the big cop's deep brown eyes. As she looked into them, she saw the pain and anger residing there. She also saw the honesty. "How do you know it's a man, Captain?"

"I don't," he said. Then he broke the stare, hesitated, and turned his head away. "But how do you know it isn't?"

"I don't," Jill said. "Not yet."

She stood, offered her hand, and smiled. Auxton shook her hand. Then she left his office the way she had come in, and the stares from the narcs there needled her. She made her way to her car—on loan, compliments of Alabama's governor—and headed out into the traffic.

A block from the police department office, a strange sixth sense told her someone was watching her. And that thought not only frightened her, it made her skin crawl.

A fish had taken the bait and was running with it.

Maybe.

Chapter Five

□ □ □

"Delta Force, huh?" Bubba Ray said. He sat relaxed across the room from the Highway Warriors in his dockside office. "Well, ah s'pose that explains why you boys fight like a coupla tigers. So now you drive them eighteen-wheels. Hmm."

"Keeps us on the move," Carl said. He had already pegged Miles as a die-hard bigot, but he played along anyway. "We're not inclined to let moss grow under our feet, if you know what I mean."

"Yeah," Marc said. "It's not always easy gettin' a paying gig when you got a dishonorable discharge swinging from your back."

Bubba Ray bit down on his cigar. "Boys, ah got to tell you, yo' story sounds just a mite farfetched. Ah got to admit, though, ah ain't never seen nobody fight quite the way you do. What kinda work you lookin' for?"

"Drivin' . . . or whatever is available," Marc replied. He tilted his head slightly to one side to indicate the broad scope of his proposal. He hoped Bubba Ray was buying it. Right now he wasn't sure, but he was determined to make the sale.

"Dock work?" Bubba Ray asked.

"If that's all you got, we could do that awhile. I'm not sure how your boys outside would take to it," Marc said with a sarcastic laugh. "But I'll tell you one thing, Mr. Miles, we can flat-out roll some rubber over white lines if there's anything like that available."

"You boys wanted by the law for anythin'?" Bubba Ray asked.

"Not that we know of. We're just on Uncle Sam's shit list, that's all. We did our time for what they said we did in the service."

"Why heah? Why me?" Bubba Ray asked suspiciously.

"Like we told you," Marc said. "The guys down at the I-ten truckstop said you might be the man to talk to."

"You know we had us a little problem over heah the other night, don't you?" Miles asked.

"We heard," Carl said. "That don't bother us at all. We don't have any great love for the feds since we got screwed by Uncle Sam's army. I wouldn't care if they all got blown away."

"What part of the country you boys like to drive?" Miles asked.

"Wherever there's a delivery," Marc replied. "We'll go anywhere and haul anything if the price is right."

"Aw right, ah'll tell you what," Bubba Ray said. "You boys leave me yo' full names, social security number, birthday, and yo' driver's license numbers so's ah can make the necessary checks. If you come back to my likin', ah'll put you to work. Where can ah get in touch with you?"

"Well, Mr. Miles, uh, how long is all that gonna take? We got to get to work, and if it's not here, then we got to find someplace else," Carl said excitedly.

"Keep yo' zipper up there, boy," Miles said, and he shot a mean look at Carl. "You come back to see ole Bubba Ray tomorrow mornin' and ah'll have you a answer one way or another."

"We'll be in the rig or the motel at the I-ten truckstop," Marc said. "You'll be able to reach us there if you send somebody for us. Otherwise, we'll be back here in the morning. What's a good time for you?"

"Seven o'clock," Miles said. "You be here then if you ain't heard from me beforehand."

"We'll be here, Mr. Miles," Marc said.

The Warriors left the information Miles wanted and left by way of the dock. Angry, menacing stares followed every step they took, but no one dared to push his luck a second time. Not yet, anyway.

When Marc and Carl were clear of the dock, Bubba Ray hollered into the next room. "Ronnie, did you get all that on tape?"

Ronnie yelled back. "Got it, Bubba Ray."

"Good, now come in here and get this information. Get on the horn to our boy at the po-leese department and check these scoundrels out. Ah think they're revenuers of some kind. Ah want to know everything there is to know about 'em. Ah need that information back in heah before nightfall. If they're federal boys, then we'll skin their hides and hang 'em out to dry. If they turn up clean, then we'll hire 'em and put 'em to good use."

Jill made a left turn, drove one block, and made another left. She inconspicuously glanced at the rearview mirror, careful not to turn her head and reveal her intent. She saw nothing unusual, but she still felt it. Something, some internal alarm, kept telling her someone, some*thing*, was watching her.

She drove another block and made one more left turn. Another glance into the rearview mirror revealed nothing. She couldn't see the tail, but still, she knew they were there somewhere.

She made it back to the main highway that she had been on before she made the left turns and picked up her original direction. Once more, she glanced inconspicuously into the rearview mirror and saw nothing out of the ordinary.

She thought about radioing Brittin Crain or Harvey Harrison, but decided against it. They were, after all, watching her on the "bird." The sophisticated electronic system monitored every move she made through the earth-orbiting ComSat-D satellite system's transponder tracking window. There were two transponders. One had been installed in the frame of the loaner car, and the other one, smaller than a paper clip, was attached to the inside of her bra strap at the front snap. Both were activated to transmit simultaneously and thereby give Crain and Harrison comparative signals to determine her exact physical location should she have to leave the car for some reason. But even with the sophisticated monitoring system, the stark reality remained that should she encounter trouble, she was on her own until backup could get to her. And that, she knew, could take time. Vital time that could prove fatal if the scenario unfolded the wrong way.

Jill checked the rearview mirror again and this time she saw it. A red Pontiac Trans Am with two occupants. She had seen the car earlier, but it hadn't followed her through the tactical sequence of left turns. But it was there now, a half-dozen car lengths back in the traffic. The driver had apparently waited, knowing the full intent of her turn sequence, and picked her up again when she came back out on the highway.

Okay girl, time to think. Remember the training in Georgia. Play it by the numbers. Do it right the first time.

Traffic ahead was heavy, almost bumper to bumper. The highway was five lanes. Two lanes permitted travel east and two west. The fifth lane was a left-turn lane divided by double yellow lines on each side. But now she could see clearly to the traffic signal a block and a half away. There were three cars in the center lane signaling for left turns after the green arrow lit. Jill reduced her speed, hoping this would be exactly what her pursuers expected her *not* to do. She counted quickly. There were twelve cars in front of her in the left lane. The right lane was blocked also, but she was still half a block from the red light now and cars drifted to a stop. She counted down, waiting for the traffic light to turn green.

It did.

Jill floored the accelerator and the Dodge's engine roared as her sedan lurched forward. She cut hard left and entered the center lane. Streaks of black rubber scored the pavement behind her. She reached the intersection and the last car in the left-turn lane turned out of her way. She bored through the intersection, cutting back hard to the right in front of the traffic waiting for the light to turn green for the eastbound lanes. Then she grappled with the steering wheel and straightened the car in the center of the two eastbound lanes. Fifty yards ahead, the lanes were stalled with two cars stopped in each lane. Jill cut right beside a utility pole and ran on the sidewalk until she cleared the blockage. The she cut back onto the pavement amid a scream of sliding tires and blaring car horns. She reached another intersection, tapped the brakes slightly, then flew ahead of cars crossing the busy highway from the side street.

A quick glance into the rearview mirror revealed the Trans Am weaving in and out of traffic like a snake on hot sand. The red car was still a half block behind and threading through the startled traffic with great difficulty.

Jill looked again to the highway in front of her. She slammed on the brakes and cut hard to the right to avoid a car stopped dead in front of her. The sedan hit the curb and rocked onto the sidewalk with a thunderous jolt. It narrowly missed a large steel sign pole, but clipped the leading edge of a U.S. Postal Service drop box. The heavy blue steel box flew violently from its anchors and went sailing in the midst of strewn concrete chips and scattering airborne mail. *That'll piss off the postal inspectors*. But the thought had little time to register before the car sent mass-transit patrons fleeing a bus-stop bench. The last person jumped to safety a microinstant before the front fender engaged the concrete lip of the bench's seat. Like the mailbox, the bench left its anchors and tumbled into crunched concrete waste as the car tore through it and continued out into the street.

The Dodge rocked and groaned, then skidded sideways under the stress of excessive torque. More black streaks marked her trail as Jill straightened the Dodge and hit the accelerator hard, pressing it to the floor. She swerved to avoid a blue pickup truck that entered the intersection at the same time she did. The driver of the truck, a young woman with straw-blond hair, hit her brakes, sounded her horn, and flicked a finger at Jill in undiluted anger.

The Trans Am was still back there. It wove through the wave of destruction with delicate caution and reduced speed, but it was still only a half block back. Not nearly far enough for a clean escape from the grips of whatever the driver and the passenger had in mind for Jill. And that was a thought she didn't have time to concentrate on right now either.

Jill's Dodge cleared the intersection and shot forward, fishtailing. Jill fought the steering wheel and straightened the car. Traffic had thinned now and she had a clear shot through the next intersection that would take her onto Interstate 65. She plotted her course. Seconds passed as the Dodge chewed pavement, then the entry ramp to the interstate highway was on top of her. She tapped the brakes and cut the steering wheel sharply to the right. She entered the ramp and floored the accelerator again.

The Trans Am held steady, closing slightly, and homing in on Jill's Dodge.

When she finally made the right lane southbound, she checked the rearview mirror once more and saw six eighteen-wheelers coming on close from the north. The end of I-65 was only a few miles ahead and that meant she had to make a decision. She could merge with I-10 to the west and go on into Mississippi or cut right on 10 east and try to make the preestablished rendezvous point and notify Crain in the process.

She chose the latter.

Behind her now, the eighteen-wheelers had both southbound lanes full, effectively blocking the Trans Am. Jill moved into the left lane and prepared to enter I-10. She glanced into the mirror again and the Trans Am was visible. The driver had swerved into the emergency lane on the shoulder and he was overtaking the eighteen-wheelers. The sound of air horns blared behind her. But the Trans Am was undaunted. The driver cut back onto the highway in front of the lead rig.

Jill hit the ramp and merged with Interstate 10 eastbound. She knew that would take her by the docks and the shipyards that lined the shores of Mobile Bay. It would then take her across the bridges and through the narrow tunnels that spanned Mobile Bay and onto dry land on the east side. But there was no choice. One thing was certain; she couldn't let them catch her on the bridges. A hit there would be a matter of simple calculation. All the attackers would have to do would be to ram her and send her car careening over the retaining walls into the salty water below.

Jill fumbled in the seat beside her with her right hand while she steered with her left. She found the familiar case of the Icom U-16 transceiver. She lifted the radio slightly and placed her thumb on the transmit switch. She felt her way over the DTMF keypad on the front and found the "#" button without taking her eyes off the highway ahead. She keyed the transmitter and pressed the "#" button at the same time. She held it that way for at least ten seconds. The radio transmitted both the RF and the audio tone signal. It would be received by Crain and Harrison or one of their men at the temporary command center across the bay from the anchored USS *Alabama*. The tone signal was a preestablished alert that indicated trouble. The contingency plan then called for Crain and Harrison to meet at the rest area east of Mobile Bay unless they received a second tone, in which case, the FBI would close in on the location indicated by the transponder's signal.

Jill didn't send the second tone. She already had a plan if the players in the Trans Am decided to carry on their game.

They did.

Jill shot a fast glance at the mirror and saw the Trans Am closing hard as she entered the first small tunnel leading to the bridge system that crossed the wavy waters of the bay. When she cleared the other end and came out into the sunlight again, the Trans Am was only two car lengths back and holding steady.

Jill shot through traffic, oblivious to the low retaining members that joined together to provide a slight margin of safety for vehicles on the massive bridge structure. She moved in and out of traffic, weaving her way toward the east side and the rest area where she hoped Crain and Harrison would be waiting.

The Trans Am moved in closer now with only one car separating it and Jill's battered Dodge, then shot into the clear lane and moved in for the kill. The Dodge and the Trans Am snaked through traffic on the bridge span as if they were attached by a tether. Tires screamed and the cars protested under the strain of violent, unexpected turns as they dodged traffic and streaked toward the east side of Mobile bay.

The end of the bridge was a half mile away. Jill saw her chance. Two eighteen-wheelers were in the right lane, bumper to bumper. The one in the rear had his left-turn signal flashing to change lanes. She watched as it moved out of the right lane to overtake the vehicle ahead of it. She quickly checked the rearview mirror and saw that the Trans Am had backed off slightly. The driver was apparently holding back to see what her next move would be.

Perfect.

Jill focused ahead at the big truck and pressed the accelerator to the floor with such force that her leg throbbed. She gripped the steering wheel tightly and held her breath. The Dodge moved into the slipstream of the eighteen-wheeler coming into the left lane and then shot past it, almost scraping against the retaining wall in the process. Jill mentally felt the impact . . . but it never came.

The startled driver of the eighteen-wheeler yanked on the cord to sound the air horn and swerved hard to the right to avoid hitting the Dodge. The instant Jill passed, he cut back into the left lane to avoid colliding with the other eighteen-wheeler. When he did that, he effectively cut the Trans Am off. The driver of the eighteen-wheeler looked into the mirrors and saw the Trans Am close hard on his rear bumper. By then, he was somewhere between scared and completely ticked off. He looked to the other driver, beside him now in the right lane, and lifted his CB microphone. He pressed the talk switch and spoke. "Sorry about that close one, Mr. Trans America. The skirt in the Dodge just about bought me there. Thought fer sure I had her. We got us a hot cowboy on the back door in one of them souped-up Fire Chickens. What say we just back 'em down and let him boil? I think he was chasin' the skirt."

"Roger that, Mr. Big Yellow," the driver in the right lane said. "I thought the skirt had nailed your tail for a second there. I'm backin' down on this side. If that cowboy back there don't like it, let him swim to get around us. Let's us see what that Fire Chicken looks like when the driver's boilin', huh? Handle here is Apple Jack. We be out of the big D-town in Texas."

"Yeah, Mr. Apple Jack. Roger-four on that one, guy.

I'm a backin' down over here, too. You got the Mean Machine out of Baton Rouge in the yellow cab headin' east to Tallahassee and feelin' sassy."

"Yeah, roger, Mr. Mean Machine. Let's coast the cowboy to the other end of the bridge. If he's in that big a'hurry, he can grab himself some median when we get to the end, huh?"

"Uh-huh, ten-roger on that. He wants to get feisty when we get to the end of this bridge, I'll feed him a tire iron for lunch," Apple Jack said.

"Look at that crazy character back there," Mean Machine said. "He's like a pissant in a pepper box."

Apple Jack glanced at his rearview mirrors and watched as the driver of the Pontiac Firebird Trans Am swerved from lane to lane. He kept his horn blaring constantly and flashed his headlights on and off. He was less than five feet off the rear bumpers of the eighteen-wheelers. "Hey, Mr. Mean Machine, reckon what that cowboy would think if I just sort of tapped the brakes a little while he's tryin' to kiss my backdoor?"

"Careful, Mr. Apple Jack, you wouldn't want Fire Chicken lip prints all over the backside of your pretty, big truck now, would you?"

Apple Jack keyed the microphone and laughed. "Yeah, roger-four on that. Where'd the skirt get to?"

"Boy, she was hammer down and she just rolled off at the exit up ahead."

The end of the bridge appeared and the rigs rolled onto solid ground at the same time as white lines zipped behind them.

Apple Jack pressed the talk switch and glanced at the Mean Machine saddled in the cab of his big eighteen-wheeler beside him on Interstate 10. "The cowboy's takin' to the shoulder. He sure must want that skirt real bad, huh?"

Before the words cleared his lips, the Trans Am was

past both eighteen-wheelers. The driver headed for the exit ramp and closed fast on Jill's fleeing Dodge.

Jill caught a slight glimpse of the Trans Am as it sped along the shoulder and headed off the highway. She looked ahead, saw a parking lot and the facilities there, and then she spun the Dodge to a stop between other cars. The instant the engine died, she jumped from the door and ran toward the first building she saw. She quickly scanned the area for any sign of Harvey Harrison or Brittin Crain. She saw neither or any car she recognized that would indicate they were there. And that sent a bolt of fear-filled lightning through her. As she ran, she moved her hand into her purse until her small fingers wrapped around the grip of the Beretta 92-F Compact. She reached the building and glanced over her shoulders. The Trans Am sat in the parking lot near her Dodge. She did a double take, because there was no one visible in or around it. She stopped and looked over the area carefully, but saw no one.

Jill walked quickly to the door of the building, and just as her hand reached for the door handle, a cold voice from behind her sent chills up and down her spine. All she heard was "stop."

She spun around, her finger moving gently back on the trigger of the Beretta inside her purse, and saw a man and a woman staring into her eyes. It took only a microinstant to see they had no weapons showing, but there was a determined look filling both of their faces. "Who are you and what do you want?" she asked as authoritatively as she could.

The woman was slender, probably five-five, and not over 110 pounds. She wore tight jeans and a loose button-up top. Her hair was glistening black and long. She looked at Jill and their eyes bored into each other with penetrating fire. "I'm Dianne Oakley and he's Benjamin Jasper. We want to talk to you alone. Now."

"What about?" Jill asked. Her finger stayed on the

trigger and she could tell the hammer was halfway to the cycle drop point on the double-action automatic. She held firm, ready to kill the man first. Then she saw hope and slowly shifted her instinctive aim toward the woman.

The man identified as Jasper was in his midthirties, clean cut and muscular, with dark hair. He answered, his voice icy and firm. "Believe me, it would be in your best interest to talk to us now. Alone."

"You can talk to me alone," Brittin Crain said through clenched teeth when he appeared without warning. He pressed the muzzle of his Smith & Wesson 1006 10mm automatic against the back of the man's head and eased back on the trigger. "Or I could just splatter your brains all over this sidewalk and save the lip service. What'll it be?"

Chapter Six

Carl let the Leeco high-tech overroad rig coast into the parking lot of the truckstop on I-10 near the Mississippi state line. "What do you think?" he asked. "Will Miles take the nibble and give us a chance to set the hook?"

Marc scanned the trucks in the lot, rubbed his chin, and smiled. "When his source, whoever that might be, runs our statistics through NCIC or military computers, I think our boy will be elated. With the information planted there by Harrison and Crain, we're going to come off like prince royal bad boys. Desperate ones at that. It should toss us right up Bubba Ray's alley."

"Think he'll send somebody over here for us today or wait to see if we show tomorrow?" Carl asked.

"Oh," Marc said, "he'll wait. He'll want us to squirm a bit before he takes us in. If he comes off overly zealous, it wouldn't look good for his 'Mr. Big' image. I saw right off that good ole boy Bubba Ray likes to be in control. That's what makes him tick."

"I'll take your word for it," Carl said. "And if that's the case, let's go inside and get a cup of coffee and wash up. I feel dirty from walking around in Miles's dump." He shut off the engine and removed the keys from the ignition.

"Sounds good to me," Marc said. He lifted his shirt to inspect the position of the Smith & Wesson 5906 9mm automatic concealed there. "I'm ready whenever you are."

Carl opened the door and climbed from the cab. Marc removed a small transmitter from his shirt pocket and set the alarm system on the rig. Then he took a final look around the lot and walked toward the truckstop restaurant.

"Why do I feel like I'm being watched?" Carl asked.

"Probably because we are," Marc replied. "My guess is Miles has eyes all over this part of the world. I'd bet the dope business for this truckstop is all his or one of his cronies. My gut tells me Miles will know everything we do between now and the time he makes his move to contact us. Just consider the next twenty-four hours a test and I think we'll do all right with Mr. Bubba Ray Miles."

The Warriors reached the restaurant and, after a brief stop in the men's room, settled at a table and waited for the waitress. When she came, Marc and Carl ordered coffee. They watched the nameless faces seated around the large room. Men and women who rolled eighteen wheels across the blacktop and concrete trails of America delivering the wares that made the country turn.

Carl focused on Marc's face. "You know something, bro, it never ceases to amaze me that men and women so dedicated and so necessary for the existence of this country and its life-style are so frequently treated with so little respect by the average Joe. People just don't understand what it takes to roll a big rig from one side of the country to the other."

Marc nodded in agreement. He looked around at the faces, watched them as they ate or sipped coffee. "Holds true for many professions. The ones who are the most necessary are sometimes the least respected. People take them for granted. Truckers have, from time to time, taken a bad rap. It isn't the many who cause it either, it's the few. All people ever hear are the horror stories about the ones who create havoc in a crash or some act of horror. They're good people, these truckers. Most of them, anyway. Decent people who drive for a living to support families. They do what most people won't to earn their living. Worst part is, sometimes they suffer from an image problem because of the irresponsible acts of a few in their ranks. Like most of life, the bad acts make the news. The good deeds go unnoticed. Damn shame, too."

"Given time, maybe that, too, will change," Carl said. "Miles is using truckers to haul his synthetic death around the country. The preliminary reports told us that much. Surely those drivers who work for him know what they're doing. I don't think they can plead innocence by ignorance. That's the kind of thing that hurts every man and woman sitting in a cab."

"That's exactly what we have to stop here. Miles and his kind have to be removed from the midst of society by whatever means necessary. It's not an easy task. It may not even be workable. To get them all, that is. But every one we can eliminate is one less thorn in the ass of decent people everywhere."

Carl tapped Marc's foot under the table as he looked into the restaurant. "Behind you at three o'clock. We got us a deal goin' down."

Marc continued to look the other way. "Are you sure?"

"No doubt about it. The guy with the long hair and faded jeans. He's coppin' a deal with the two men at the booth."

"What did you see?"

"He slipped a bag from his pocket and slid it under the table to the man in the corner. The one in the red plaid shirt. Wait, here it comes. He just took some folded bills and stashed them in his pocket."

"Get a good look at him," Marc said. "I think we need to sit tight for now. We take the slime down and we could blow our cover along with our chance at Miles."

"Affirmative," Carl said.

"You keep the booth warm. I'm going to the rig and

activate the HDTV. We can run it until this guy leaves and get him on tape. Might be something we could use for future reference. If he's working this turf, he's got to have ties to Miles."

"Do your thing," Carl said.

Marc left the table and went immediately to the Leeco rig. He deactivated the security system and climbed aboard the cab. Once inside, he switched on the electronics console and punched in the activation code for the high-definition television cameras. He activated the electronic pan control and set the sequence with a digital encoder. Once that was up and running, he entered the sequence on the computer keyboard to activate the Ampex multitrack videotape recorder. When he was satisfied that the systems were functioning properly, he climbed from the cab and headed toward the restaurant again.

Marc noticed a faded green van parked across the lot. He saw two men inside it, but they did nothing out of the ordinary that he could see. He took his eyes off the van and continued walking. But then his sixth sense screamed an alarm. He didn't know why, but something in his gut was yelling at him. Warning him of danger.

He kept walking. The van was behind him and to his right now, but his internal alarm continued to sound. What he couldn't see was the barrel of the scoped high-powered rifle protruding slightly through the side window of the van, or the chiseled face of the man whose finger squeezed gently on the trigger. Nor did he understand that the internal alarm was telling him the cross hairs of the telescopic sight were lethally aligned on his head and death was just a heartbeat away.

Bubba Ray Miles possessed the cunning of a fox and the survival skills of a coyote. He let those instincts, honed by generations of Miles family heritage, control his actions, and they had told him the best place for him to weather the latest storm was at his isolated farm north of Mobile. He had left Miles Shipping and Drydock Company minutes after Marc Lee and Carl Browne. Ronnie Richardson drove the Cadillac Fleetwood and Joe McNally rode shotgun in the front passenger's seat. Miles sat in the back and watched the landscape as the car devoured broken white lines en route to his refuge.

Miles lifted the handset of his cellular telephone and punched in a number. Seconds passed, then the phone rang on the other end. When a man answered, Miles spoke quickly. "Todd, you got any word back on my request yet?"

"It's working. I expect something in hand very shortly. Where are you?"

"In the car on the way to the farm. We're on Route forty-three south of McIntosh. We ought to be there in fifteen or twenty minutes. Get mah Jacuzzi warmed up fer me. Ah need to relax when ah get there. Ah want to know which trucks and how many we got road-ready. We got some serious business to attend to before the day's out."

"I'll pass the word and see that it's done," Todd said. "Anything else?"

"No. Wait, yes. Put a bottle of mah best homemade wine on ice. Ah want that while ahm relaxin'," Miles said.

"Done," Todd replied.

"Good," Miles said. He replaced the handset in the cradle and looked back out the window. His mind wandered, plotted.

Joe McNally glanced into the backseat. His voice growled, deep and loud, when he spoke. "Bubba Ray, them two guys that come to the dock today, you think they're legit?"

"Dammit, Joe, ahm right here," Bubba Ray snapped. "You don't have to talk like ahm hangin' off the back bumper. To answer yo' question, ah don't rightly know. If they check okay, then ah might think about 'em. They're the fightin'ist two scoundrels that's been in these parts in a mighty long time. Ah got to give 'em credit fo' that."

Ronnie Richardson broke his silence. "I don't trust those guys, Mr. Miles. They're trouble. I can smell it on them. Something ain't right. They come prancing down the dock like a couple of heroes and beat all hell out of half of our longshoremen. Timing just ain't what it ought to be. You know what I mean?"

"Yes, sir, ah know," Bubba Ray said softly. "Ah was thinkin' that very thing mahself. First thought that came to mah mind when ah first seen 'em. But that's okay. They want to come to work for us and they check out okay so's they ain't no more heat comin' down on me, then ah just might put 'em to work. We'll put 'em out where they can't do no harm. Ah got a special test all lined up iffin they come with us. Of course, if they don't check out okay, then they can get a big ole dose of the same medicine we give them other revenuers and we'll be shed of 'em."

"What sorta test, Mr. Miles?" McNally asked.

"Ah'll put 'em on the road with some other boys and give 'em just enough rope to hang themselves real good," Miles replied.

"Our dock workers aren't gonna like those guys much, Mr. Miles," Richardson said. "Not after what they did this morning."

"Not a problem," Bubba Ray said. "They don't have to like 'em. All they got to do is load them trailers so we can get our goods rollin'."

"If you don't mind me saying so, Mr. Miles, those two guys make me real nervous," Richardson added. "Like I said, something about them just ain't right."

"Them revenuers been nosin' their way into Miles family business for years and years, Ronnie," Bubba Ray said. "Ain't never been one of 'em get close enough to do us much damage. We got generations of dodgin' them suckers. It's in our blood. Ain't no trick they can play that some

Miles, sometime, ain't seen before. We can handle anythin' they's capable of dishin' out. Besides that, we got us somebody on the payroll with ears hearin' everything that's goin' on with them law people."

Richardson watched the road and alternated his glance from the windshield to the rearview mirror, where he watched Bubba Ray in the backseat. "Bubba, things have changed today. It's a changin' world. It's just not like it used to be in the days of running moonshine. This dope business is different. Technology is the name of the game. They got everything on the side of the law, except maybe the law itself. They got listening devices that's so sophisticated it takes an electronics genius to figure them out. And phone taps, shucks, a kid in school can put a tap on somebody's telephone. There's satellites that can show the cars in your driveway and then count the heads inside your house with that infrared stuff. I'm thinking maybe we need to put some more thought into what we're doing. We got the resources to make a good countermove on these feds and local lawmen. We need to spend some money and get even in the technology department. You can't just do it with guns and street smarts anymore."

Miles stared into the rearview mirror and saw Richardson's face there. He didn't speak for a long moment, but the sound of his breathing filled the car. He turned his gaze from the mirror and watched the scenery outside the car windows when he spoke. "Ronnie, we might not be as dumb as you think we are. There's a lot of stuff you and most of mah other people don't know about. When we get to the farm, ah'll take you for a little walk into some parts of the farm you and Joe ain't never seen before."

"What are you saying, Bubba Ray?" Richardson asked.

"Ahm sayin' that maybe ah ain't quite as dumb as people think ah am. The Miles family didn't survive in Alabam all these years by bein' dumb. We may not have our walls full of them fancy de-plomas, but we ain't all that dumb neither. When you got enough money, you can buy yo'self somebody to do them things fo' you." Miles looked again into the rearview mirror at Richardson and his face split wide with a smile. "You got a grip on mah drift, Ronnie?"

Richardson smiled also. "Yeah, Bubba Ray, I think I do."

"I don't think I do, Bubba Ray," McNally said. "Did I miss somethin'?"

"That's all right, Joe," Bubba Ray said. "It just sailed right over yo' head. Ah'll show you, too, when we get to the farm. You won't be left out. Ah promise."

Ronnie Richardson negotiated the Cadillac along Alabama Route 35 west of McIntosh. The land was quite flat, but dotted with a heavy covering of trees. Most were small or scrub brush, but they were dense. That made the terrain difficult to negotiate on foot and contributed substantially to overall security. The highest point in Washington County was High Hill at 266 feet above sea level. Settlement along the narrow county road was sparse and that was one of the things that had attracted Miles to it many years before. Although the terrain wasn't too hilly and heavily forested like that of central and northern Alabama where the Miles family had endured generations of hardships in illegal manufacture and sale of moonshine, it provided an isolated refuge for the new generation of drug marketing and distribution. In the drug business, isolation was a blessing and secrecy a necessity.

The driveway to the farm departed Route 35 to the right and wound north through dense brush for almost a mile. The narrow drive was built of "penetrated concrete"—a concrete base sided and topped with creek or river pebbles worn smooth, polished by the natural currents of the stream. At the end of the driveway nearest the house, a guard shack held a security man. Entry could be attained only through the heavy steel gates. The gates were controlled by the guard or from a control inside the house, which sat another two hundred yards beyond the guard shack on the other side of a dense growth of scrubby trees. There was also a small transmitter similar to a garage-door opener inside the Cadillac to let Bubba Ray operate the gates without the inconvenience of stopping each time he came in or out.

The gates came into view. Richardson pressed the switch on the transmitter and the massive steel twin structures moved outward. Richardson waved at the guard, a man obviously cut from the same cord of wood as the men who worked on Miles's docks, and the Caddy slipped past the shack toward the front of the house. When he turned the car into the final stretch of driveway, he turned left, went immediately to a covered portico on the left end of the house, and stopped beside the French doors.

Joe McNally was out of the car almost the instant it rolled to a stop. He opened the rear doors and Miles slid across the seat and stepped out. "Ronnie, you and Joe come on inside. Ah got somethin' in heah ah think you boys might ought to see. It's part of mah su'prise for them two rounders."

Richardson removed the ignition key and followed McNally and Miles into the house. They walked through the den into an alcove at the rear of the house that had always been off limits. Bubba Ray opened a door and glanced down the steps that led into the basement. He looked back at McNally and Richardson. "This here's mah special pardy room."

"Uh," Richardson mumbled. "I didn't know there were basements in this part of the country."

"Ain't many with the water table bein' so close to the top of the ground and all," Bubba Ray said, smiling. "But this here's one of 'em. Cost me a small fortune just to get this here thing built and waterproofed. Ya'll ain't never seen this place before, have you?"

McNally and Richardson shook their heads in unison.

"Well, come on down," Miles said. He started down the steps with McNally and Richardson behind him. "This heah's where Todd spends most of his time. We got stuff down heah like nothin' you boys have ever seen. Necessary stuff we use almost ever' day in the business."

Miles led them down the steps and then through a maze of concrete-walled corridors until they reached a heavy steel door marking the entry into another section of the basement. He stopped, pressed a button on the intercom, and spoke. "Todd, it's me, Bubba Ray. Hit that there button and open the door."

No reply came through the speaker, but a buzzer sounded and the door automatically broke free of its latch. It opened an inch and Bubba Ray grabbed the handle to open it the rest of the way. He gestured for Richardson and McNally to enter.

Once they were inside, the door closed behind them. Richardson's mouth dropped open when he looked around the room. McNally stood speechless. He saw it, didn't understand it, and felt himself completely overwhelmed at the awesome display of lights, switches, computers, display monitors, radio and communications receivers, and telephones.

"Welcome," Todd said. "This is the nerve center for Mr. Miles's operations. We can operate our drydock business, trucking operation, and other related enterprises from the confines of this room."

"Yeah," Bubba Ray said. "Ah originally had it built for a bum shelter. Since we ain't had no bums fallin' from the sky lately, we converted it to a more profitable use. Man can come down heah and stay for a long, long time if he wants to. We got beds, a bathroom, and a kitchen over on the other side. This here's Todd's playroom. He takes care of all mah businesses from heah. 'Course ah keep mah eyes on him pretty close."

"I've been with you for five years and I had no idea," Richardson said.

"Uh-huh," Bubba Ray replied. "Not too many people know about this. And this heah's the place where ahm gonna put them two boys to test. You know how?"

"No," Richardson said. "How?"

Bubba Ray grinned, looked away, and lit a cigar. He trashed the burned match and pointed to the computer screens lining the console to his right. "If we put them boys on the road, ah can talk to mah trucks from right heah. Ah'll know ever' move they make the minute they make it. If they mess up or try to stick it to ole Bubba Ray, then ah'll personally send 'em both on a permanent one-way trip straight to hell."

Chapter Seven

Brittin Crain's deep, authoritative, Southern drawl was filled with the fury of a blizzard. "Hot dog, you blink your eyes the wrong way and your final lesson will be an education on what a forty-caliber, one-hundred-and-eighty-grain hollow point does to brain tissue when it passes through it at sixteen hundred feet per second."

Benjamin Jasper didn't move. His eyes were wide as saucers and filled with terror. "Be cool, man. I can explain this."

"Explain it from the ground," Crain said harshly. "Get to your knees and put your hands behind your head with your fingers interlaced. Be smooth, hot dog, or it's bye-bye time."

"You too," Jill said to the woman. "You heard the man. Do the same thing. My hand isn't inside this handbag just to keep it warm. Get cute on me, honey buns, and the first one goes right between your boobs."

Dianne Oakley obeyed and dropped to her knees.

Jasper did the same thing.

Crain had stepped back when Jasper moved. But now he moved forward and kept the Smith & Wesson out of Jasper's reach. He leaned over and patted Jasper down with his left hand. He hit the butt of a handgun on the guy's right side. His hand went immediately under Jasper's light jacket and unsnapped the retainer strap on a large automatic pistol. He lifted it free of the holster and brought it into the open. "Good taste in handguns, hot dog. A Smith & Wesson 4506. Let me guess, you got the paperwork for concealed carry and this is for protection because of your job, right?"

"Almost," Jasper said. "I'm a cop. We both are."

"Cops?" Jill said. "You sure as the devil don't act like cops. What's your beef?"

"No beef," Oakley said. "We know who you are. Everybody in the department knows who you are. We want to help you find the people who killed those officers. Those men were our friends. Problem is, right now we don't trust anybody in the police department. You being from outside, we thought maybe we could trust you unless your job is to come in here and do a massive whitewash job."

"Okay," Jill said. "I'm still listening. So who am I?"

"You're Sergeant Jennifer Lane. You work directly for the governor," Jasper said.

Jill shot a glance toward Brittin Crain, who still stood poised to deal a death hand if the situation warranted it. Crain nodded his head in a way Jill took to mean that he wanted her to keep the pair talking.

"You're doing good so far," Jill said. "Tell me one good reason why I should believe your story. How do you convince me that you're not one of the sources for the leak that cost those men their lives? How do I know you aren't as dirty as tanker bilge?"

"I guess you don't," Oakley said. "Maybe if you gave us half a chance, we could convince you."

"Oh, you convinced me, all right. You convinced me you're up to no good. Your approach leaves a lot to be desired. If you're who you say you are and you followed me for the reasons you say you did, why didn't you just come clean and tell me who you were from the beginning."

"Trust," Jasper said. "We know somebody is dirty.

Somebody leaked information that got those men killed. We want a stab at whoever it is. When we're finished with them, you can have what's left and prosecute them for as long as you want. We want in on the takedown, that's all."

"Not good enough," Jill said. "Care to try again?"

Jasper looked into Jill's cool blue eyes. "Dianne was engaged to one of those men who got his tail shot off on Bubba Ray Miles's dock. They were going to be married in two and half months. She's got a personal interest in this one. Like we said, we felt like you being from the outside, maybe, just maybe, we could trust you. I apologize for scaring you like we did. We're pretty damned scared right now ourselves. We still have to work in that department and we know some clown made a sellout. We want justice. That's all we want."

"Where's your ID?" Crain asked Jasper.

"In my left hip pocket. Want me to get it out for you?"

Crain snickered. "Hot dog, I wasn't born yesterday. I think I can manage. Officer Lane, if this man twitches the wrong way, kill the woman and then blow his tail away."

"Gladly," Jill replied.

Crain moved a step forward and patted Jasper's hip pocket. He found the outline of what felt like a wallet or badge ID case. He moved his hand into Jasper's pocket and lifted the ID case out. He flipped it open with one hand and read the ID inside. "Okay, so the ID looks authentic. I'm still not convinced by your story. I think your modus operandi speaks much louder than your feeble words."

"Look," Oakley said. "We know the intricate details of Miles's shipping-and-trucking operation. We know he was behind the massacre. We just can't prove it. We've got information it could take you people months to acquire. And while you're wasting that valuable time, the tipster is still on the inside feeding Miles with every move you or anyone else makes."

"I'll bet you do," Crain said. "Somebody sure knew the

ins and outs well enough to get fourteen cops killed. O
course, if you worked for Miles, you *would* know that kin
of information. I'm still not buying it."

"Come on, people. What in God's name do you wan
us to tell you that will convince you?" Jasper pleaded.

"We can talk about that on the way to our lockup," Ji
said.

"I agree," Crain said. "Let's cuff 'em and take 'em for
ride. Get her weapon and then search hot dog for a backup
piece. I'll cover you."

"You can't arrest us. We haven't broken any laws,"
Oakley protested.

"Nobody said anything about arrest," Crain countered.
"We're just going to take you two out of circulation for
little while."

"That's illegal. We may be cops, but we've got ou
rights just like anybody else," Jasper said angrily.

"Good," Crain said. "Since you know about you
rights, there won't be any need for me to go through all the
Miranda scenario, huh?"

"You can't do that," Oakley said.

"Oh no, you got that all wrong," Crain said. His voice
remained low and cool. "We not only *can* do it, we're *going*
to do it. Finish the search and cuff 'em, Sergeant Lane."

"Lane, who is this clown?" Jasper asked. "He hasn't
bothered to identify himself."

"Name's Crain. FBI."

"FBI?" Oakley said.

"Did I stutter?" Crain asked.

"FBI. Governor's Task Force. What is all this?"

"If you're clean and our inquiries substantiate that,
then you'll be free to go in a few hours. If you're not and the
facts say you're hot, then this is your time of accountability.
Your final judgment."

"What does that mean?" Jasper asked nervously.

"It means our rule book doesn't read quite the same way yours does," Crain replied.

"Wait a minute," Jasper said. Now he was very nervous. "Who are you people really?" He paused as the answer suddenly hit him like a baseball bat on the bridge of his nose. He took a deep breath and immediately realized he was extremely afraid. "Oh God, you're some kind of kill squad or assassination team or something, aren't you?"

"Something," Crain said without emotion. Then he pulled the Smith & Wesson Model 100 handcuffs from the small of his back with his free hand and clamped the first one around Jasper's wrist. "You see, we know who we are and what we're after. Within the next couple of hours, we'll know the same thing about both of you. You can count on it."

The restaurant door opened and Marc stepped sideways, yielding to allow the exiting patron to get outside before he entered. In an eyeblink, glass shattered and lethal shards flew in every direction. A microinstant later, the sound of a gunshot roared across the parking lot.

Marc went instinctively low and rolled across the sidewalk, fisting his Smith & Wesson 5906 halfway through the roll. He stopped on his stomach, elbows propped on the concrete, and searched for a target, the source of the hostile gunfire.

The second shot sent chips of concrete and lead fragments flying in a deadly hailstorm. Marc caught a glimpse of the gun barrel reflecting in the sunlight as the shooter recovered from the rifle's recoil. The guy was in a van across the parking lot. Marc fired the first shot double-action, and a heartbeat later the second semiautomatic round roared from the Smith. He followed that with a pair of double taps. Then he rolled again, an instinctive evasive action, and crawled on his belly through the shattered glass to the front door of the restaurant.

The startled but unhurt patron had ducked back and disappeared inside.

Carl had heard the gunshots and was crouched in the doorway now just inside the restaurant. "You okay, bro?" he asked as Marc slipped past the shattered door.

"Yeah," Marc answered. "Shooter's in the green van across the lot. He's got a scoped rifle and a nervous finger. I felt the wind from that one."

Before Carl could make an effective judgment, the van roared and the vehicle lurched forward, leaving streaks of smoking rubber on the pavement in its wake. Marc dropped to his knees and slipped the barrel of the powerful automatic through the jagged glass left in the aluminum door frame. He steadied his aim with a reflexive two-hand hold on the autopistol's grips and fired three fast semiauto scorchers at the van's right front tire. It ruptured with a resounding pop.

Carl stood against the cover of the door frame and unleashed six rounds of 9mm hellfire into the van's windshield. The van stayed fixed in the lethal sights of the Novak three-dot sight system on the top rib of the autogun as balls of white-orange fire streaked from the blazing muzzle. Hot brass flew rapidly from his Smith & Wesson 5906 as spent shells pelted the walls of the entry alcove then tumbled to the floor.

The van streaked across the parking lot, dodging eighteen-wheel rigs and seeking a path for escape. The windshield had collapsed inward from the impact of Carl's scorchers. It remained mostly intact and lay at an awkward angle across the passenger compartment like a sheet of stiff plastic with road-map etchings across its surface. The pressure of the glass slab against the steering wheel presented a difficult obstacle for the driver to overcome. That, coupled with a flat front tire, caused him to lose control of the speeding van. It careened right, snaked farther across the lot, then fishtailed left. The driver stopped for a second, reevaluated his escape plan, then floored the accelerator again. The van fishtailed a second time and moved in a beeline across the lot toward the restaurant door.

"He's coming in," Carl yelled.

"Let's get out of here," Marc replied. He leaped through the door and landed on the glass-covered sidewalk, with Carl right behind him.

Both Highway Warriors rolled and came up on their feet in a crouch, their autopistols firing streaks of blazing death toward the van. But even against a fusillade of hot lead, the driver of the van was undaunted. He was fifty yards away, the green machine zigzagging across the pavement like a panic-stricken snake.

"Make a run for the rig," Marc yelled. "I'll keep them distracted so you can make it."

"Got it." Carl rolled left and ran as hard as he could toward the Leeco rig parked a hundred yards away.

Marc kept his attention on the van. It swerved now, it's left side facing him. The shooter appeared on the opposite side and leaned from the passenger's window with the high-powered rifle. The guy tried to make a clean shot at Carl, but Marc sent another burst of 9mm sizzlers into the body of the machine. The Federal Hydra-Shoks easily ate metal and chewed into the interior of the van, leaving gaping holes in their path. The shooter ducked back inside without firing a shot.

Marc reached into the small of his back and retrieved another magazine for the Smith. He hit the magazine release on the left side of the grip frame and dropped the empty stick. He caught it with his left hand and then slapped the full stick up the beveled well. He gave it a sharp rap with the heel of his left hand to be sure it had bottomed out and locked into place. Then he thumbed down the slide release on the left side of the frame and the slide slammed into battery, taking with it the first deadly round from the top of the magazine. He came on-line with the van again and touched off a roaring double tap.

The van swerved left and returned to its course toward Marc and the front of the building. The right front tire, previously penetrated and deflated by Marc's bullets, was disintegrating now. Shreds of rubber sheathed the steel rim of the wheel and clapped into the metal framework of the van with each rotation. The van listed to the right, and the driver fought to retain control as he continued the deadly onslaught.

Marc popped off another three-round burst and the sizzling projectiles hit the engine compartment cover. Paint chips and fragments of copper-jacketed lead sprayed from the front of the van, but the driver kept on his course of imminent destruction.

Carl was near the rig now. He ran hard for his survival and Marc's. When he was thirty feet away, he activated the pocket transmitter to disable the rig's security system. He manipulated the short digital code to unlock the cab doors electronically. When he reached the rig, gunfire raged behind him at the restaurant. Carl glanced over his shoulder to satisfy himself that Marc was still okay, then hit the running board on the fly and grabbed the door handle. The door swung open and he quickly climbed inside the Armorshield safety of the cab. As he slammed the door behind him, he fired the massive Caterpillar diesel powerplant. Precious life-threatening seconds passed while the engine roared and warmed. Carl activated the weapons systems controlled by the electronic console between the driver and passenger seats. The computer screen came to life with a color display and the beep of the scrolling RAM memory initialization check.

Carl slipped the rig into gear and popped the clutch. The Leeco machine groaned and leaped forward amid a cloud of diesel smoke. Carl floored the accelerator, cut left toward Marc, and shifted gears. The optic sight for the

Stinger miniguns came on-line with the assaulting van, but Carl didn't fire since Marc was also in the lethal coverage area of the impending fusillade.

The severely crippled van was almost on top of Marc now. The Highway Warrior rolled to his left, toward the Leeco rig, and fired out the remaining rounds in his second magazine. The slide on the third-generation Smith & Wesson locked open. March reached for his last magazine in the small of his back, but there wasn't time to make the change. He held the Smith tightly and rolled again. This time, he felt burning in his arm and leg where sharp shards of glass cut into his skin. He came out of the roll at the instant the van should have hit him. It didn't. Instead, the driver hit the brakes and the green machine slid, fishtailed left. The rear left edge of the van caught the leading edge of the doorway alcove into the restaurant. More glass and long strips of aluminum sailed toward the ground. The driver recovered control and hit the gas again. The van screamed more streaks of rubber on the pavement before it finally caught with enough traction to gain solid forward momentum.

Marc saw his chance. The driver's door was only feet away from where he now crouched. The van raced toward him in a deadly assault. Marc slammed the 9mm into his waistband and made a maddening leap toward the driver's door. He caught the door handle with his right hand and thrust his left fist through the open driver's window. His fist landed a glancing blow to the driver's cheek. The guy fell back in the seat from the impact, but he kept the accelerator floored. Marc held tightly as the van gained speed and crossed the parking lot toward the Leeco rig.

The driver zigzagged now, swerving to try to shake Marc's hold from the handle.

It didn't work.

Marc held on for his life. His feet slapped and bounced against the pavement as the van gathered more speed. Pain crashed through his legs and streaked through his body, but he kept relentlessly pounding at the driver's head. All the while, he tried to keep from losing his grip on the door handle. His body flew like a windsock now, hitting and bouncing and then hitting the pavement again. Each time the pain became more severe. Then the driver shoved open the door. Marc dangled more precariously now as the door opened and closed with the vibration of the van. He could see the passenger inside the van with blood streaking down the side of his face from a gash above his left eye. The guy was fumbling with the scoped high-powered rifle and trying to get it pointed at Marc without having the driver in his line of fire. The muzzle finally came up and Marc knew there was no place to hide.

Carl could see it all with both his natural eye and the computerized optic sight. He moved a finger to the firing mechanism, but he still couldn't fire because the heavy firepower built into the rig covered too broad a path for a safe burst of machine-gun fire. But there was a chance, albeit remote. Carl dropped the firing mechanism and reached behind the passenger seat for his silenced Uzi. He found it and braked hard. The big rig slowed. Carl opened the door, then shifted the Uzi to his left hand. He steered with his right and leaned standing from the cab through the open door. He took aim with the Uzi and tapped off a burst directed at the van's passenger. Tongues of bright fire spat almost silently from the Uzi's muzzle with little more noise than the clapping of hands. The scorching death fliers intended for the passenger impacted the cracked sheet of safety glass that had once been the windshield. They struck at such a precarious angle that they ricocheted off the glass and into the van's ceiling.

Marc held tightly as the ride punished him and pressed his hand, arm, and shoulder muscles to painful new limits. His left arm, the one he had tried to beat the driver with, was now draped over the lip of the window in his best effort to sustain his hold on the door. He looked inside and saw that the passenger had the rifle pointed directly at him. Marc kicked hard and the door made another open-and-close cycle before the hinges sent it back toward the framework of the van. When he looked piercingly into the wild eyes of the passenger, he saw the reflection of cold death there.

The driver was pressed firmly against the seatback now in anticipation of the shot and the very dangerous muzzle blast that would streak across in front of him. That compounded the already difficult job of steering the van.

A fireball appeared from the muzzle of the scoped rifle and Marc felt the concussion as it slapped into him with violent intensity. There was no sound, only hellish ringing in his ears. The only thing he could think of was the peculiar theory that the victim never hears the shot that kills him. Then he could see nothing and feel nothing. His grip slipped from the door handle and he felt himself falling, the pavement rising up to meet him. Although it was the bright light of midmorning, there was nothing except darkness. And in that instant Marc Lee knew the grim reaper of doom had harvested him.

Chapter Eight

□ □ □

Benjamin Jasper could hear Dianne Oakley breathing, but he couldn't see her. She was to his left in the brig lockup twenty or thirty feet away.

Several cells, all of them empty, separated them. He had seen that much when Crain and the woman he knew as Sergeant Jennifer Lane had locked him away. The pleas hadn't worked and neither had the threats. He had quickly learned how difficult it is to make a threat bear sharp teeth when the other guy has the gun and your hands are cuffed behind your back.

He strained to see through the aged bars of the lockup. He could see the microphone and the device he suspected, knew, was a transmitter. That meant Lane and Crain were monitoring every word spoken inside the brig. Water slapping into her side caused the USS Alabama to sway lazily. The beat of the small waves against the hull of the retired battleship was the only sound, besides Dianne's breathing, that breached the haunting silence and resonated throughout the cavelike brig.

Jasper wasn't sure how long they had been detained in the cells, or even whether the sun still shone outside. Aside from a small, dim lamp that burned in the walkway in front of the cells, there wasn't the slightest trace of light. But that really didn't matter. What did matter was that the killers of the lawmen on the docks of Miles Shipping and Drydock Company were still free and waiting for another opportunity to kill other men. That and the drugs. While precious time passed, Bubba Ray Miles took the opportunity to dispense his synthetic death to tortured souls who thrived on his wares. That chemical madness lined his pockets with twenty-four carat gold and made the recipient of the temporary euphoria a little more dependent on Miles with each dose.

Benjamin Jasper knew he had to do something and do it soon. He decided to try talking again. He spoke in a loud voice, almost yelling. "Crain, listen to me. I know you can hear me. I want to talk to you. We're letting valuable time slip away. You've got to let Dianne and me out of here. We can help you. Come down here where we can talk."

"You're wasting your breath," Oakley called into the walkway from her cell. "I can read his eyes. He won't let us out of here until he's damned good and ready."

"What's with this guy?" Jasper asked. He directed the question at Oakley, but he wanted Crain to hear. "I'm not convinced these people are who they say they are. I think they're in on the Miles deal some way."

"No," Oakley said. "I've heard of units like this. I never thought they really existed until now. The name Crain still rings a bell from somewhere. I can't remember where just yet. Seems to me there were more people involved with him. He wasn't the headliner, so to speak. Do you remember anything about something in Louisiana or somewhere else in the South? Maybe a year or two ago."

"Doesn't hit me," Jasper replied. "But then that doesn't mean anything. I can't even think right now. It pisses me off, Dianne. We're locked up in here and Miles is shipping death all over the country while we sit with our hands tied. Maybe we should have just acted alone, you know, just done what we know has to be done to get to the bottom of this and put Bubba Ray Miles out of business once and for all."

"You're talking crazy, Ben. That's not the way this country operates. God knows, sometimes I think it might be a better place if it did. You're right about the pisser, though. Here we are, the ones trying to end this insanity, and we're locked up, hands tied, so to speak, and the real villains are loose on the street. What does that tell you about justice in this country?"

Jasper shook his head in disgust and then slapped his hands into the cold steel bars. The sound echoed throughout the brig. "Crain, we've got to talk to you. Please."

"Crain, you and Sergeant Lane please listen to us," Oakley added. "We've got information that can help put this thing in wraps, but we can't help from here. You've got to let us out or at least talk to us," she pleaded. As soon as she did, she wondered why she wasted her voice and her strength.

"Face it, Dianne," Jasper said. "They could leave us here until we rot and no one would ever be the wiser. They obviously have the cooperation of the tour people on this tub. All they have to do is make this section completely off limits and we could stay here forever."

"Save it, Ben. It's no use. They'll come for us when they're ready and not before," Oakley replied. "Maybe they'll do their homework and realize we're straight."

"Yeah, and maybe they won't," Jasper said. "Maybe they'll get bad information or they won't look in the places that support us. Maybe they'll even talk to the person Miles has in his pocket. If that happens, then what?"

"How long before we'll have concrete information back on those two?" Jill asked. "They're getting on my nerves." She glanced at the external speaker attached to the hand-held radio that received the signal from the transmitter belowdecks.

"Any time now," Brittin Crain replied. He sat at the laptop computer and pushed keys. The LCD display was filled with data from Jasper and Oakley's employee files. "Nothing yet that even suggests anything except truthfulness. Let them chatter down there. It'll give them something to do while we wait. You know, I hate this part of the job."

"Maybe they were telling the truth," Jill said.

"We've got people working on it," Crain said. "Shouldn't be too much more legwork and some answers will come in. In the meantime, I think we'll sit tight. I've got people assigned to the dock area to keep those eighteen-wheelers under surveillance. Those things move out and more illegal drugs hit the streets. Miles may be a good ole Southern boy, but he's got the cunning of a fox. He's capable of anything. You'd think that all this heat on his operation would slow him, but it hasn't. He's running with all engines full speed ahead."

"How's he getting everything into his warehouse without somebody nailing him?" Jill asked.

"I don't know. That's one I was hoping Marc and Carl could answer," Crain said. His eyes never left the computer screen while he spoke. "If they can get inside and we can continue to gather external intelligence, I think we can fold this thing up before too long. It's a shame people like Miles use truckers like they do. Most drivers, men and women, play by the rules. They're straight and just trying to make an honest living. Enter a man like Miles, and the good guys get tempted by big bucks. All they have to do is put one more carton on a trailer and make a run to wherever it is they were going anyway. I see how they fall, but it sure gives the industry a bad rap."

Jill looked at Crain. For a long moment, she caught herself slipping away into the past and the events of savage brutality that had brought her to this moment. "It sure hurts Marc, I know that much. He's spent most, no, all of his life in or around the trucking industry. To see the process unfold right before his eyes . . . wow, I know it hurts. It used to be bennies and yellow jackets just to keep awake on a cross-country long haul. It's gone so much further than that now."

"Yeah, and to think someone like Miles gets richer by the day off of the lifeblood of hardworking people. To tell you the truth, Jill, it makes me want to throw up."

"Speaking of Marc and Carl, have you heard from them this morning?"

"Yes, about an hour before I got your call. They had their meeting with Miles and it went just like we expected. They had a major altercation on the dock and whipped the pants off of a clan of Miles's hardcore killers. They went to the truckstop out on I-ten to sit tight and see what develops. They're waiting on Miles to run a history on them. Maybe that input will give us the data we're looking for. It could tell us who the dirty cop is. We've got their criminal history red-flagged. Of course, we planted just what we wanted in the file. Miles's man, or woman, makes the inquiry and we've got us a scent to follow."

"From what I understand about the system, there are a number of ways an inquiry could get in without the person we're looking for actually touching the chain. What if it's a dead-end street?"

"Then it's one more street we'll walk down until we reach that dead end," Crain said. He looked up from the computer for the first time since Jill had initiated the conversation. He crossed his arms across his chest and took a deep breath. "We'll know everything there is to know before we give up on the lead. We can't let anything go by without thorough investigation. Enough lives have been lost trying to take this slimy heathen. We won't let him walk away. We can't."

"Ah want all the available drivers in here within an hour. We need to sit down and have us a little chitchat before ah send them out there on the highway. We got us a lot of work to do and they ain't much time to get it done in," Bubba Ray said. He sat in the den of his home at the farm north of Mobile.

Ronnie Richardson looked at him conspicuously. "You want to have them come *here*? Isn't that risky?"

Bubba Ray sipped on a glass of brandy, then lit a cigar. He sat the glass on an end table and settled back into his favorite chair. "Why? Ain't nothin' heah nobody can make no case on. This here's just mah home. Ah'd be plum nuts to keep anythin' heah. Ah just want to have me a little conversation with the drivers. Ah want to know the best ones and the worst ones. Ah got to know who I can trust and who ah can't. If ah look 'em right square in the eyes, ah can tell if they're bein' honest or tryin' to pull the wool over mah eyes."

"Okay," Richardson said. "You're the boss. I'll get the calls out and have them come here."

"You do that," Bubba Ray said. "Ah'll be waitin' in mah hot tub sippin' on a jug of mah best stock. When we get them drivers heah and get 'em lined up, we'll get all them ludes we got stored out of the warehouse over on Pleasant Street. They ain't makin' me no money sittin' in cardboard boxes over there."

"What about the cops? They're watching every move we make. We all know that," Richardson said.

Bubba Ray took a long draw on his cigar and smiled. "Ain't no big deal, now, is it? Ah mean they was watchin' us at the docks the other night, too, wasn't they? What'd it get 'em?"

Richardson just looked at Miles and said nothing.

"Ah'll tell you what it got 'em. It got all of 'em dead. They keep messin' with Bubba Ray Miles and they'll be a lot more of 'em dyin', too."

"Okay," Richardson said. "I'll leave that to your judgment. I'll make the calls." He stood and walked toward the door that led to a small alcove near the back of the den.

"Ah'll be in mah hot tub," Bubba Ray said. He took another long draw on the cigar and then drained the glass of brandy. He held it in his mouth and swallowed it in one big gulp. Then he looked at Richardson and grinned. "Before you get on that telephone, find one of the girls and send her back to mah spa. Ahm in the mood for some lovin'."

Marc's feet slapped brutally into the pavement. The impact was so hard that it ripped the sole loose from one of his boots and sent it catapulting end over end across the pavement. His arm was still draped over the open driver's window, but his grip was gone from the door handle. His right arm dangled loosely beside him. He had no balance, no sight, and no normal motor skills. Time seemed suspended. He could see his body, but he couldn't feel anything. It was like he was someone else looking on at his situation, detached and free from it all. His mind crashed and his head throbbed with massive bright flashes of pure white light followed immediately by cold, pitch darkness. But then his consciousness came back. Marc realized he was alive and his next conscious thought was of the intense pain that consumed his body.

The van was skidding out of control. Marc blinked his eyes, tried to focus, but his sixth sense was screaming at him and warning him of impending disaster. It took all the strength in his body to twist his head around and look in front of the van. When he did, he saw the long blunt nose of a conventional-cab eighteen-wheeler coming on fast. Marc had enough of his senses about him to realize the van was going to collide with the big truck. He made a decision and reacted as fast as his battered body would permit. His left arm was numb because the angle at which it draped over the open window had shut off the circulation. Somehow, he made it move, felt it slip from the door. Then the pavement was there, all around him. He hit with a jolt, rolled and tumbled. Pain intensified and every muscle and joint in his body ached. Then he heard the impact.

The van collided head-on with an eighteen-wheeler parked across the lot near the spot where Marc had first seen the van. The bandit green machine had come full circle, but the onslaught ended as abruptly as it had started.

Carl stopped the Leeco rig in the middle of the parking lot. He jumped from the cab and raced to Marc's side. He saw cuts and scrapes, but nothing appeared serious. He knelt beside him and spoke. "You all right, bro?"

"I'm not sure. I feel like that van ran over me. Jeez!"

Carl lifted Marc's arms. "Come on, I'll get you to the rig. We can't afford to hang around here very long."

Marc stumbled, felt weak-kneed, but managed to stand with Carl's help. He limped, staggered, back across the pavement toward the Leeco machine. When they got there, Carl climbed up and opened the passenger door while Marc kept his balance against the front fender cowling. Carl climbed back down and helped Marc make the steps until he was seated comfortably inside the cab. "I'll be back. I don't think our boys are going anywhere. If they're still alive, I want to have some conversation with them."

"I'll be okay in a few minutes. Go do it," Marc said. He gritted his teeth between bursts of pain.

Carl climbed from the cab and went directly to the van. When he got there, he found both occupants unconscious in the front. Blood trickled from open wounds and ran down their faces. Carl pried the passenger door open and grabbed the high-powered rifle from the floorboard. He laid it on the pavement and went immediately to the passenger. The guy was big, probably six-three or -four. He was still alive but there was a large contusion on his forehead where he had apparently sustained a blow during the crash with the eighteen-wheeler. He left the guy and went to the driver, who was slumped over the steering wheel. His bleeding face rested against the leading edge of the ruptured windshield. Carl grabbed the man's hair, lifted his head off the windshield, and studied the guy's face for a long moment. A stream of blood had already dried and caked along the side of his face. Carl checked the man's carotid artery for a pulse. There was none.

Carl let the dead man's head fall back against the windshield. He went back to the passenger. He lifted the man out of the seat and hauled him to the back of the Leeco rig. He laid him on the pavement and triggered the transmitter in his pocket to open the rear doors. When they opened, he carried the guy inside the trailer and took him to the living quarters. Once inside, he gagged and bound the man to be sure he didn't go anywhere or cause any further damage, then he rifled through the man's pockets and found a brown wallet. He flipped through it and located a Mississippi driver's license. He stared at the name, Thomas Barton, then tucked the license into his shirt pocket. He glanced down at the unconscious man. "Well, Thomas Barton, I'm taking you for a ride."

Carl turned to leave when he heard a sound behind him. He jerked around. Barton was stirring, beginning to regain consciousness. Carl stepped back in front of him and waited. When the guy managed to lift his head, Carl reached down and grabbed a handful of hair. He tugged without compassion and the guy's eyes shot open. They immediately filled with fear.

"Well, Mr. Barton," Carl said. "You're not having such a good day. First you got your butt whipped on Miles's dock and then you came back for a second dose. You a slow learner or what?"

Barton's eyes widened. "Where's Billy Dugan?"

"If that's the clown driving the van, he wasn't quite as

lucky as you. He ate a windshield for midmorning snack. He's dead."

"Who are you guys?" Barton asked.

Carl smiled, his teeth showing white behind his dark lips. "We're the nightmares you had as a kid and the fears you keep hidden as an adult. And besides that, we got a real bad attitude when it comes to scum like you."

"What are you gonna do? I need a doctor."

"In time," Carl said. "Right now, you and me gonna talk. Here's how it works. I ask the questions and you give me the answers. If I don't believe you or I don't like your answer, then I take my fist and work on your face a little bit. What do you think?"

Barton was trembling. "You're crazy, man."

"Yeah." Carl smiled. "And don't you forget that. Now you tried to kill me and my partner. I know you work for Miles Shipping and Drydock Company. Did Bubba Ray Miles or one of his sidekicks send you?"

"I ain't sayin' nothin' to you, nigger."

Carl shook his head in disgust. He looked away for a second then jerked around quickly. His right hand flew out and backhanded Barton across the face. Barton's head jerked hard against the impact and fresh blood appeared. Carl grabbed Barton's hair again and held it with his left hand. He drew back a clenched right fist and pulled tightly on the blood-matted hair. "Now, see, you've started off with a real bad attitude. This is my attitude adjustment instrument."

Carl slammed his fist into Barton's face with all the force he could possibly deliver. Barton's head snapped back and blood splattered into the air. It took a long moment for Barton to recover. He coughed and blood dribbled from his smashed lips. A tooth dangled from his bleeding gums.

"Now, see, boy, that's how I change attitudes. Do you like it?"

Barton shook his head no.

"Good, 'cause that's exactly what you're going to get every time I have to ask the same question twice. Maybe, if you live, you'll change your mind about answering me before you slip away into unconsciousness again."

Barton was in extreme pain. He fought to retain consciousness and keep breathing. "Miles didn't send us. He'd probably kill us if he knew we did this."

"You're lucky, boy. I like it. Where is Miles?"

"He left just before we came here. Right after you and the other fella did. He's gone home."

"Where's home?"

"A farm north of Mobile out in the country."

"How nice. Why did you try to kill us?"

Barton choked, cleared his throat, and answered through swollen lips. "The men were all pissed off because of what you guys did on the docks. We drew straws to see who'd take you out. Me and Dugan got the job."

Carl laughed. "You been gettin' tough breaks all day long, haven't you? About those killings at the docks. We've heard a lot of rumors and no substance. Were you there?"

Barton hesitated and renewed fear lit his eyes. He didn't know whether to answer the question or take another beating. He decided not to press his luck. "We all were. Miles made us. It was a setup from the git-go. You're a cop, ain't you?"

"No, I'm not a cop. I'm a trucker. Was Miles there? Did he know what was going down?"

"Hell yes, he was there. He even killed a couple of 'em hisself. He set the whole thing up. He knew that Baxter fella was a narc. We all did. If you ain't no cop, what difference does all this make to you?"

Carl chuckled. "None really. But I got some friends that are going to be real interested in what you have to say. Now, one little word of warning. When my friends talk to you, you give them the runaround or play word games with them and I'll come visit you in your cell. When I'm finished, they'll have to scrape your face off the walls. Any questions?"

Behind a mask of blood and fear, Barton shook his head. There were no questions. None.

"Good," Carl said. "This might prove to be your lucky day after all. You might get to live."

Chapter Nine

Benjamin Jasper jerked upright on the cot inside his cell when he heard the clang of the heavy metal door opening. He ran to the front of the cell and gripped the bars that separated him from freedom. Through the echoes in the walkway, he heard Dianne Oakley stirring in her cell. Neither of them spoke when Brittin Crain and Jill Lanier, still known to them as Sergeant Jennifer Lane, entered the walkway.

Crain stopped at Oakley's cell, Jill behind him. He lifted a key from a heavy brass ring and inserted it into the cell-door lock. The sound of the heavy steel tumbler falling echoed throughout the brig. "Detective Oakley, you may come out now."

Oakley didn't speak. She dropped her hands from the cold steel bars and walked through the doors. She stopped beside Jill and looked at her carefully in the dim light.

Crain walked to Jasper's cell and repeated the procedure. When Jasper was clear of the lockup door, he ran toward Oakley. "Are you all right, Dianne?" he asked without even acknowledging Crain or Lane's presence.

"Yes, I'm fine," she said. Then she turned to Crain. "What now? Do we just walk out of here and pretend none of this ever happened? Do we ignore a blatant violation of our civil rights?"

"No," Crain said. "You come to work with us. The necessary arrangements have been made with your department." Crain reached behind his back and removed two handguns. "Here are your weapons. I suppose this is where I should tell you that on behalf of the United States government, we apologize for the inconvenience. Hopefully you will understand that your detention was necessary to verify just which side you were operating on. We have verified that to our satisfaction. It appears you were telling the truth. If both of you are willing to shove your egos aside, maybe it's time we go upstairs and have a long talk. We have a lot of work to do and very little time to get it done. What say?"

"I say you got a lot of balls, Crain," Jasper said as he accepted his pistol. He tucked it away in its holster and adjusted the ride until it was once again comfortable. "I've worked hand in hand with a lot of federal agents in my time, but I've never seen one that operates quite like you do. Are you a gutsy renegade or is this kind of behavior sanctioned?"

"Like I said, we have a lot to talk about. We need to know everything you people have on Bubba Ray Miles. We need any information on the dock bloodbath that might have slipped through the reports. Are you willing?"

Oakley forced a grin. "Somehow I get the distinct feeling we have no choice, willing or not."

"You're a perceptive officer, Miss Oakley," Jill said.

"You're not so bad yourself. You led us straight to Crain when we came after you, didn't you?" Oakley asked.

"You got it. We aren't amateurs, Dianne. We take care of our own," Jill said, smiling. "We have determined there is no room for error in this line of work. A bullet is a terribly unforgiving competitor."

"Let's go to the captain's quarters and I'll buy you two a cup of coffee," Crain said. He moved toward the heavy steel door that led to the narrow stairway and the upper deck.

Dianne Oakley followed him on the steps with Benjamin Jasper directly behind her. Jill brought up the rear just in case the two Mobile PD officers had a sudden change of heart about cooperating.

It took five minutes to weave through the maze of corridors, locks, and doors to the captain's quarters. They went inside and each person took a seat.

"I just got one question," Jasper said. "How did you guys pulls this one off?"

"What?" Crain asked.

"How did you get control of this ship?"

"Easy, you just ask the right people. The exhibit is closed off a few days for what we shall call scheduled maintenance. Let it rest as an application of proper bureaucratic influence."

"I'm impressed," Oakley said. "This is the last place I'd ever figure to find a special operation headquartered."

"And I'm sure this strategic location has nothing whatsoever to do with the fact that you have a clear line of sight to the water side of Miles's shipping facility," Jasper said.

"You're catching on," Jill replied.

"Pretty clever," Oakley said. "Who would ever have thought to use an old retired battleship for an op post. What other tricks do you people have up your sleeves?"

"In time, Detective Oakley, in time," Brittin Crain said. "For now, let's just draw the line on questions. It's our turn. I need to fire the tape recorder and have some conversation with you. We need to know everything you know about Bubba Ray Miles."

"You mean you don't already have it?" Jasper asked.

"Probably," Crain said. "But you never know when somebody somewhere missed something. I'm of the opinion that it never hurts to compare notes. You might have a special link or a tiny shred that will tie other loose ends together. This is going to become a complicated case if we don't get more concrete evidence against Miles. When we take him down, I want the case open and shut . . . airtight."

Oakley looked around the quarters at the stacks of computers and communications equipment. "What does it take to haul off this stuff, a trailer truck?"

"Something like that," Crain replied. "Remember, it's our turn to ask the questions."

"Shoot," Jasper said.

"Okay," Crain said. He shot a glance at Jasper, then fixed his eyes on Oakley. "Why don't you two just give us the *Reader's Digest* version of what you have assembled on Miles. You might also give us some insight on who you think the leak on the inside might be. Anything new would be a great help."

"You want to go first, Dianne?" Jasper asked.

"Okay," Oakley said. "Where do you want me to start?"

"At the beginning," Crain said.

"All right, the vice units of Mobile PD have been stalking Miles for more than six years. There's always a path, but never a solid trail to his doorstep. That is, no one has ever been able to make a case. We know he's using a fleet of eighteen-wheelers to haul his wares. Most of the drivers are hired hands, but some are independents he uses without their knowledge from time to time. He brings the drugs in from somewhere in the north. We suspect Michigan, but again, no one has been able to prove it. Miles has a complex distribution network that we feel operates out of his shipping business. It's just a scam. He does just enough other merchandise handling there to cover his tracks and keep the heat off. We think he's responsible for the deaths of more than a dozen informants over the past three years. We know beyond a doubt that he's the one who master-minded the murders of the Mobile and federal agents on his docks a few days ago. We haven't been able, though, to get anyone on the inside of his shipping system, that is the trucks, long enough to make a solid case. You must remember that Miles is an old-line Alabama moonshiner who has no respect for the law or representatives of authority. He has even less respect for the value of human life if that life jeopardizes either him or his operation. He's a man guided by his own pathetic greed. He has neither morals nor compassion. He's an animal who must be caged if we are to ever clear up the massive drug trafficking in south Alabama and the Gulf. More than anything, Miles is a—"

The sound of a voice crackling over the speaker of a two-way radio sitting atop one of the desks in the quarters interrupted Oakley's commentary. "Surfsider, this is Pathfinder. Do you copy? Over."

Brittin Crain looked at Jill Lanier, then at the radio. "I'll get it," he said.

"Okay," Jill replied.

"Excuse me just a moment." He moved to the radio equipment and fisted a handheld microphone. He depressed the talk switch on the side and spoke slowly. "Pathfinder, this is Surfsider. We are ten-twelve, but we copy. Over." He knew Marc and Carl would understand the ten-code that indicated a visitor was present. He also hoped they would choose their words carefully when they talked.

"Roger, Surfsider. We are too. Got a little package for you all neatly bundled and tied in ribbons. I think it's one you'll appreciate. Seems to have a lot of knowledge about current events. With the right motivation, he seems to have a lot of parakeet in him. He likes to sing. We're headed for a date north of Mobile. Think we can get together before we go that way?"

Crain thought he understood, but he waited to let the conversation settle in his mind. He pressed the talk switch again. "Roger, Pathfinder. We can make arrangements to eyeball. You name the place. It's your game."

"Roger," Carl said. "We got a few bumps and bruises on this end. Marc isn't having one of his better days. How about we make the gift transfer at a rest area?"

"Anything serious?" Crain asked. He glanced over his shoulder and immediately noticed that Jill had tensed.

"Negative. Nothing some R and R won't take care of. Might also require a few Band-Aids. Pick the spot."

"Okay," Crain said. "Make it the first rest area east of the bay. That seems to be a popular one today. Do I need anything special for this bird?"

"Negative. He could probably use some stitches and a couple of ice packs. His health has taken a sudden turn for the worse in the past hour or so," Carl said.

"I understand," Crain said. "What's your ETA?"

"Fifteen minutes tops. Could be less depending on traffic. Why the ten-twelve?"

"I'll get into that when we make the meet. Unless you got anything further, we'll see you in ten to fifteen. Sergeant Lane will also be with me. Is that affirmative?"

"Affirmative," Carl said. "You might also be aware that Mobile's finest are probably looking for us. We had a little misunderstanding at the truckstop. We had to leave them a cold one there. One of our boy's best hired hands. Might not be a bad idea to get the man at the top to filter the word down and suggest that they don't look too far or too hard. You catch that?"

Crain shot a glance at Jasper and Oakley. He hesitated before he answered. "Affirmative, got it."

"I'll also give you some personal statistics to run when we meet. Okay, we're heading for the heavy traffic near the tunnel. See you in a few. Pathfinder clear."

"Surfsider clear. See you." Crain laid the microphone down on the table and looked at Jill. Jasper and Oakley stood with their mouths open.

Oakley spoke first. "Don't tell me. I think I get the feeling we really don't want to know. Am I right?"

"Right," Jill said. "Some things in life are better left unsaid. This just happens to be one of them."

"What are you people, CIA or something?" Jasper asked. "This isn't like any police operation I've ever seen. And believe me, I've seen a truck load of them."

"We're not CIA," Crain said. "We're just out here doing a job. Matter of fact, most of our people come from the trucking industry in one way or another. Most of us just have a few special talents that we didn't want to see grow stale. Let's let it drop. It would be in your and Miss Oakley's best interest. The less you know, the better off you'll be. Just rest comfortable in the knowledge that we are after one thing and one thing only. Justice."

"So are we," Oakley said. "I told you before, one of the people Miles and his hoodlums killed was my fiancé. I loved him very much. I won't rest until the people responsible for his death and the deaths of the other men on that surveillance team are rotting in hell."

"Neither will we, Detective Oakley," Jill said. "You can bet your badge on that."

Oakley's eyes reflected hurt and sadness. She bit her lip and fought back tears. She took a deep breath and stared into Jill's blue eyes. "I already have, Sergeant Lane."

Finding Bubba Ray Miles's isolated farm wasn't easy, but Carl finally spotted the long winding driveway that disappeared through the dense underbrush. Marc was sleeping, recuperating from the beating he had taken at the hands of Miles's thugs in the van. Carl had made the meeting with Brittin Crain and Jill. Thomas Barton had been deposited, quite unwillingly, into their care. He was now well on his way to isolation in the same cell where Crain had detained Jasper and Oakley.

Carl stopped the rig and examined the detailed map displayed on the color computer screen. No doubt about it, this was the place. He reached over and nudged Marc gently on the shoulder. "Hey, bro, we're here. You need to get yourself together. How are you feeling?"

Marc shook himself awake, although it took some effort. He looked out the windshield and then at Carl. "Like I've been beaten and left for dead," he replied. He sat upright in the passenger seat and looked around. "Where are we?"

"Best I can figure from the information we transferred into the computer, that's Miles's driveway right up there." He pointed to the paved drive leading off the main road.

"Wonderful," Marc said. He stretched hard and flexed his aching muscles. Then he rubbed his eyes and yawned. "Sorry I haven't been much help. That little skirmish at the truckstop took more out of me than I thought. What's the plan?"

Carl stroked his chin. "Looks like it's right up the middle. I don't see any other way to make the necessary impact and not jeopardize our operation. We want to get inside and firm up the case against Miles. Even if Barton rolls over completely, we still need more evidence. That's assuming, of course, this case ever gets to trial."

"That'll be up to Miles," Marc said. He was gradually coming back to life now. "I think Crain would rather see him rot in a prison cell. Anticipation makes hell a little hotter. If he plays right, we'll take it by the book. If he doesn't, then it's our rule book. The choice is all his."

"Miles ain't going to be real happy to see us burst up his turf twice in the same day," Carl said. He retrieved his silenced Uzi from behind the seat and dropped the magazine. He pushed the top round to be sure the stick was full, then he slid it back into the well and gave it a sharp rap to check that it was seated.

"Yeah, too bad about that," Marc replied sarcastically. "There's a lot of sadness in the world." He studied the terrain through the windshield. "He's got things fairly secure from the highway. If he goes off the deep end, want to just end it here?"

"Like you said, that's up to him. I say we play it by ear. I'd rather get something more concrete personally. His web of death and destruction seems to cover a large territory. When Miles goes down, I want to do everything we can to make sure that his network goes with him. The more we can get, the better."

"Okay, Major. I'm on the injured list. You call the shots and I'll ride sidekick," Marc said. He lifted his Smith & Wesson 5906 from the waist of his pants. He checked the magazine and slapped it back up the well. He inspected the spares and put them in the nylon holster at the small of his back. "Thanks for taking care of my magazines."

"Anytime," Carl said. He slipped the Uzi back behind the seat with the butt up so he could grab it quickly with one hand. He moved the strap of his musette bag containing extra magazines and accessories beside the weapon so he could grab it at the same time if it came to that. "You ready?"

"Roll 'em," Marc replied.

Carl dropped the rig into gear and pressed the accelerator. He turned the rig into the driveway and headed toward the gates of hell.

Todd knocked on the door to the glass-enclosed veranda at the back of the house where Bubba Ray Miles sat in the hot tub. "This is urgent, Mr. Miles. Sorry to disturb you."

"Why can't it wait, Todd?" Miles yelled. He held tightly to a shapely blond bombshell in the hot tub beside him. She was topless and snuggled close to him. Her hair fell in long, wet locks across her shoulders and clung sensuously to her wet skin.

"It's the report you've been waiting on about those two truckers. I just got it over the fax from downtown," Todd replied hesitantly. "I think you might want to take a look at it now."

Disgust rang clear in Miles's voice when he answered. "Oh, well, bring the thing on in heah. Now, ahm sorta busy, so ah don't want to take up lots of time with it."

Todd opened the door slowly and entered the steamy private recreation area. The windows surrounding the tub were covered in thick steam that dissipated and trickled to the floor, forming puddles of clear water beneath the window frames. The pungent smell of warm chlorinated water filled the room and almost took his breath away. Tropical plants in large wooden planters shaded the floors and walls. The floors were hand-laid slate arranged in geometric mosaic patterns that started at the edge of the hot tub and extended toward the glass walls. In the center of the artificial splendor, sat the hot tub. White bubbles rolled from the churning water below streams of steam that shot into the air-conditioned air. Miles was stretched out with one arm around his female companion and the other clutching a bottle of his best homemade wine.

"I'm sorry, sir," Todd said. "This report just seemed so incredible that I thought you would like to take a look at it. The other truckers are starting to arrive now and you might like to have this information before you make your decision on who will take which runs in the next few days."

"Ahm sorta wet, Todd. Read the damned thing to me," Miles said as he looked through the steam at Todd, standing beside the hot tub. Miles hated to admit that he had great difficulty reading, especially when it came to lengthy computerized reports. Most of the time, none of it made sense to him. But then, he reasoned, that's why he had people like Todd on his payroll.

The giggly blonde beside Miles in the tub said nothing and made no effort to conceal her breasts. Instead, she sat comfortably and smiled while Todd tried to break his eyes away from her.

Todd managed to get his eyes back to the fax sheet in his hands. His voice cracked at first, nervous. "It says those two men, Lee and Browne, were United States Army Delta Force heroes. They were hot dogs of the first class. They have both been awarded numerous medals of distinction. Their careers were off on the right track until they had a little squabble with some of their leadership team in the field. They subsequently killed their commanding officer. Shot him in cold blood from what the report says. They were tried and convicted. Sentenced to life at hard labor, but later released and discharged dishonorably. Court-martialed. Some kind of deal was made with them. Apparently the government didn't want this to get out since they were somewhere they weren't supposed to be when the killing took place. They have a rap sheet about as long as my arm. Nothing current on them, though. Nothing showing them as wanted by anybody."

"Killed their commanding officer, huh? Where was that s'posed to happen?" Miles asked. He sipped at his home remedy and then set it back on the edge of the hot tub beside the bottle.

"Central America. They were on a secret mission. One of those the military insists never existed. We aren't supposed to be able to access this information, but our source got it for us." Todd looked a little pale. "Are you sure you can trust men like this, Mr. Miles?"

Bubba Ray laughed. "Trust 'em? Hell, ah'd have boys like that in mah family. They's men after mah own heart if they behave thataway. Find them boys and get 'em in heah. Ah want to talk to 'em when ah have this heah meeting today. Ah could grow to like boys like that. 'Less, of course, they try to play some kind of silly games with me. Now, they go and do that and it's hang on to yo' backside. Ole Bubba Ray ain't gonna put up with that kind of hossplay. Them boys may be rough and tough, but ole Bubba Ray is one hell of a lot meaner. Ah can guarantee that."

Chapter Ten

Xavier "Zave" Auxton was dressed in green camo from head to toe just like the three men from Mobile PD who accompanied him. He crawled on his stomach through the dense underbrush until he reached a clearing wide enough to slip his rubber-armored camo binoculars through. He brought them to his eyes and carefully scanned the high-fenced compound that Bubba Ray Miles called home.

"What's going on there?" Sergeant Jim Kelly asked.

"Can't tell yet," Auxton replied. "There's a sea of activity. A dozen or more men milling around and more keep coming in through the gates. Miles is having some kind of meeting. That's my guess."

"Do we go in?" Kelly asked.

"Not yet. We wait. Maybe the gathering will thin out. I see Miles's Cadillac under the carport. He's here. Let's drop back and talk about it. Get DeWitt up here to keep an eye on things," Auxton said.

"Done," Kelly replied. He slid backward on his stomach until he reached the other men. "DeWitt, boss wants you on the point right away."

DeWitt, a large black man with muscles bulging beneath his camos, nodded. He lifted a black backpack and moved toward Auxton. When he reached the thick bush, he dropped to his belly and crawled up beside the captain. "What's the drill, boss?"

Auxton lowered the binoculars, but kept his eyes on Miles's house. "We got something going on down there. A lot of people arriving. My guess is Miles is getting ready to move a load of drugs and he's calling his mules in for final instructions. You stay here and keep an eye on anything that moves. Set up the parabolic listening device and tape it all. I'd like to get some conversation on tape for the record. I'm going back with the others and try to work out a plan."

"Got it," DeWitt said. He immediately unpacked electronic equipment from his backpack and assembled the components. He set up a spotting telescope on a tripod and aimed it at Miles's house, then rigged a camera to another tripod and attached a huge telephoto lens. When he finished with that, he assembled a thirty-six-inch parabolic dish, attached the microphone to the arm that extended from the center of it, and aimed the device toward Miles's house. He plugged the microphone cable into a small amplifier and distribution box and then depressed the record switch on a small cassette tape recorder.

Auxton watched a couple minutes then slipped back through the underbrush and joined the other men. He was breathing hard when he sat upright to brush himself off. "Too many people down there to hit now. DeWitt is watching and listening. We'll let the party thin out before we make a move."

"That might take a while," Kelly said.

"I don't give a damn if it takes a week," Auxton growled. "I came here to shut this end of Miles's playground down. I'm not leaving until we've done that. It's an eye for an eye. He killed our people, our brothers. They never had a chance. Now it's our turn. We'll hit hard and fast and then get the hell out of there. No witnesses. No survivors. Period."

* * *

Carl slowed the rig at the closed steel gates and eased toward the guard shack. A man, burly and weathered, stepped from the shack. He approached the rig when Carl let it drift to a stop.

The guard looked up into the cab at Carl's lean and mean face. "Boy, what the hell are you doin' bringin' that big truck in here? The boss will have a complete fit when he sees that. Besides, you're runnin' late. The other drivers are here. Have been for fifteen minutes or more."

Carl played along. "Hey, we get there the best way we can, dude. Open that steel trap so we can get this big thing settled on the other side."

The guard glanced at his clipboard and looked back up into the cab at Carl. "I need your name and the company. I thought it was only Mr. Miles's drivers comin' in here for this meeting anyway. You an indy?"

"Yeah, dude, we're an indy. Name's Browne."

The guard studied a tattered sheet of paper on the clipboard for a moment. "I don't see no Browne on this here list. No name, no entry."

"You mind if I take a look?" Carl asked. He tried to appear puzzled. "Maybe it's on there another way."

"If I say it ain't here, boy, it ain't here. But suit yourself if you wanna take a look."

Carl opened the cab door and climbed down. The guard stepped away apprehensively, but handed Carl the clipboard. Carl took it and scanned the names printed out there by a computer printer. "Hey, dude, here it is. I told you."

"Where?" the guard asked. He moved toward Carl and reached for the clipboard.

"Right here," Carl said as he held the clipboard out. When the guard's hand touched it, Carl shoved the board into the guy's chest and then backhanded him. The guard stumbled backward, lost his balance, and slumped to the ground. Carl was on top of him. He hit him again with a solid right, drew back with another, and then held it when the guard didn't move anymore. "Guess that wasn't Browne after all," Carl mumbled.

He lifted the unconscious guard by the armpits and dragged him to the guard shack. He disarmed him, tucked his liberated .357 Magnum revolver into his own waistband, and then bound him securely with a hank of rope he found lying on the guard-shack floor. He ripped off one of the man's shirtsleeves and used it as a gag. When he was finished, he dragged the guy to the underbrush and hid him well, using the long end of the rope to tie him to a tree.

The entire process took less than two minutes. When Carl returned to the guard shack, he found the switch to activate the gates. He opened them and climbed back aboard the Leeco rig.

Carl dropped the gearshift into gear and hit the accelerator. The big custom rig crawled through the open gates. The house was directly ahead. Carl looked over at Marc. He could tell the big Warrior was hurting from the beating at the truckstop. He could see it in Marc's face. He also knew they were pushing their luck pretty hard and success would require every ounce of strength and cunning they could muster. "You up to it, bro?"

"I've had better days, but yes, let's do it," Marc replied. His voice was confident, determined.

"As soon as I shut the rig off, it's into the house, taking whatever gets in our way until we find Miles. Deal?"

"Deal," Marc replied. "It might be better for us if we don't kill anybody unless we absolutely have to. You agree?"

"Agreed," Carl said. He let the rig coast to a stop beside the house. There were more than a dozen vehicles parked there. Men stood in small groups, chatting, making small talk. Carl shut off the powerful diesel engine and scanned the area quickly. He fisted the silenced Uzi from behind the seat and climbed from the cab.

Marc did the same thing.

The Highway Warriors met on the passenger side of the rig and walked toward the house. At first, no one seemed to pay much attention to them. But then, without warning, a voice shouted behind them.

"Hey, you two. Salt and pepper. What the hell are you doing here?"

Marc and Carl stopped. Carl turned and looked over his shoulder. A man, six-four and over 250 pounds, walked toward them.

Carl gritted his teeth and his jaws clenched tightly shut. "You talkin' to me, boy?"

"Yeah, *boy*, I'm talkin' to you. Who are you and what are you doin' here?"

"We came to pay a little social call on that asshole you work for."

"You ain't invited. Get your butts back in that big truck and get off this property before I have to throw you off."

"You got a name, boy?" Carl asked. His teeth shone white now. The Uzi was beside his leg, out of sight. The big man had obviously missed it.

"Yeah, black boy, I got a name. Moose. Now get your black ass back in that truck and get off this property."

"Well, Moose, since you're such a shithead, I can't do that," Carl said. He smiled and stood firm, waiting for the big goon to make a move.

"You was warned. We don't cotton to uppity niggers around here," Moose said.

"That's all right," Carl said. "I don't think too highly of lowlife white trash either. I guess we're even."

Moose growled and broke into a run. He closed the fifteen feet between him and Carl in three giant leaps. He reached Carl, throwing a right hook. Carl blocked it, stepped back, and kicked moose's feet out from under him before the big man even knew he'd been had. Moose hit the ground flat on his back in a cloud of dust, the impact knocking all of his breath out of his lungs. He gasped, breathed dirt and dust, then coughed as he struggled to get air back in his lungs. When he moved to get up, he noticed the silenced muzzle of the Uzi pressed against his nose. He froze.

"This ain't your day, white boy," Carl said. He threw a solid boot into the side of Moose's head. The big man quivered and a gush of blood rippled through his hair. His eyes closed and he didn't move anymore.

"Ain't it funny how hard the big ones fall," Carl said with a laugh.

Marc led the way into the side door of Miles's house. Carl followed, backing each step carefully. But to his surprise, he saw no one.

The Warriors started across the den. Halfway across, they switched positions. Carl led and Marc covered the back side. He reached the doorway across the room when a man with a pistol stepped out. Before the guy could react, Carl hit him with a front snap kick to the groin. They guy buckled, his fist still clutching the pistol. Carl grabbed the weapon and twisted it free. He slammed the muzzle of the silenced Uzi against the guy's ear and twisted the arm that had held the pistol until it was contorted at a very unnatural angle behind the man's back.

"Where's Miles?" Carl asked through tightly clenched teeth.

"I don't know, man."

"You people got real bad attitudes around here. One more time. Where's Miles?"

"I swear, man, I don't know. He's in the house somewhere. I just don't know where."

Carl jerked and twisted on the arm with all the strength in his left arm. A grinding, crunching sound preceded a loud pop. The man screamed as his arm went limp. "I could twist it completely off and beat you to death with it, hero. Think."

"Oh, God," the man pleaded. "Please stop. You're killing me."

"I'm not killing you yet. Right now, I'm just gonna make you wish you were dead. You got one more arm and I don't have much patience."

"He's in the back. Through these doors and down the hallway. At the rear of the house in the hot tub with some broad. Please, you're killing me."

"Any more tough guys with him?"

"Ain't nobody back there except Todd and the whore. What are you going to do to me?"

"Let you sleep. It'll help the pain go away," Carl said. He hit the guy in the side of the head and let him collapse to the floor. Blood pooled beneath his face and stained the expensive carpet.

"Still clean back here, Major. You ready?" Marc said.

"Let's go and keep it low," Carl said. "The punk was probably lying. Got to be more of them in here. Sludgeballs like Miles are incapable of defending themselves. They have to have a staff of hired thugs."

Carl worked through the hallway, searching every doorway and crevice with the muzzle of the Uzi before he moved past it. He reached the entry door to the hot tub. The wall was solid glass and covered in steam. "This looks like the place," he said. "Shall we go in and greet Mr. Miles?"

"He's probably got firepower waiting on us inside there," Marc said.

"If that's the case, he gets the very first round. You got my word on it."

"Okay, it's clear on the back side. Let's get it done!" Marc said.

Brittin Crain stood beside the cot inside the USS *Alabama*'s brig. He looked down at the battered figure of

Thomas Barton. Barton was regaining consciousness again, the second time since Crain had moved him to the brig. This time, though, Barton showed signs of remaining conscious. He sat up, used his elbows as props, and looked around the cell.

Crain stepped back and waited until the guy decided to say something.

Barton looked at Crain, scoured the room once more, and then looked at the bars. "Who are you?"

"Name's Crain."

"Where am I?"

"You're safe for the time being."

"What happened to that big black dude?"

"He's gone. You know him?"

Barton turned his head away. "No, but he's about the meanest mother I've tangled with in a while. He hits like a mule. Am I in jail?"

"Not exactly, but you are locked up. You got yourself a plate full of problems, Thomas Barton. You want to talk to me about them?" Crain decided to play it slow and easy. To make the guy comfortable and try to get his trust before he came down on him like a sledgehammer.

"You a cop?"

"Does it matter?"

"Damn straight it matters. I ain't talkin' to no cop," Barton said. He jerked his head around and stared at the wall.

"You do remember the big black man, right?"

"Yeah. How could I ever forget him? Why?"

"Well, he told me to tell you something. He said he warned you that he would come back and have another little attitude adjustment session with you if you didn't cooperate with me. Do you remember something about that?" Crain looked into Barton's eyes and smiled.

Barton's eyes spat fire through Crain. He rubbed the drying blood on the side of his face and touched the oozing wounds over his eyes. His lips hurt and he had three loose teeth, the result of Carl's massive fist striking him. "Man, I don't know what you want me to say. Besides, man, I watch television. I know I got rights. You can't do that to me. You can't make me talk unless I want to. Where's my lawyer?"

Crain's slow, deep Southern drawl roared throughout the cell. He spoke methodically, his voice low and cool. "You only get a lawyer if you're charged or about to be charged with a criminal offense. No one has charged you with anything. Matter of fact, you're free to leave any time you so desire. All you have to do is get past me and a few other people and make a mad dash to safety before someone stomps you or puts a bullet up your nose. So far this morning, you haven't done so good. Do you feel like a lucky man today?"

Barton was getting panicky. His eyes were nervous, twitching. His hands sweated and he hurt all over. "Come on, man. You can't do this to me."

"Do what?" Crain asked.

"Treat me like this."

"Okay, if you say so," Crain said. He stood and walked toward the cell door. Then he stopped abruptly and stared back at Barton, who appeared very confused. "I'd better tell you something before I go. There's a woman upstairs with a real bad attitude. Worse than yours, actually. She also has a stun gun and a forty-caliber Smith and Wesson in her purse. She's hurt and sad because the man she was going to marry in two months was one of the lawmen killed on the docks at Miles Shipping and Drydock a few days ago. And of all the crazy things, somebody slipped and told her you have some information about that. She's upstairs pleading for five minutes alone with you. Said something about shooting off your kneecaps and then your testicles until you decided to tell her what she wants to know." Crain laughed. "You know something, I think she's crazy enough to do it, too. Of course when she gets through with you, if there's anything left or you're still alive, then the big black guy wants another shot at adjusting your attitude. Wow, I hate to imagine. Well, I gotta go. Good luck."

Crain stepped through the door and pushed it closed.

"Hey, man. Hold on just a minute. You wouldn't let those people in here, would you?"

"Oh," Crain said. "I don't know that I'd let them come in if I knew about it. But I have to tell you the truth, I don't know that I'd stop them either. See you later . . . if there is a later."

Barton was wide-eyed. He gripped the edge of the cot until his knuckles turned white. His breathing was fast and irregular. "Hold it! Wait a minute, man. Don't leave me. Hey, I need help. I'm cut all to pieces and need to see a doctor. I can tell you some things, man. Come back in here and let's talk. Don't leave me to those maniacs. You can't do that to me."

"Sure I can," Crain said, and he started walking along the narrow walkway toward the stairway door.

"Crain, come back here. Crain!"

The sound of a heavy steel door slamming drowned out Barton's voice. He ran from the cot and gripped the cell bars. "Crain!"

The heavy steel door moved again. This time there was another voice. A woman.

"Out of my way, Crain. I want a piece of that animal. Let me at him just one minute. That's all I ask. Give me one minute with that creep."

"I really don't think you should do that. We'll just take him out to sea and feed his sorry butt to the sharks," Crain insisted.

"No, I want him. I want to make him hurt like I've hurt. I want to shoot him in the kneecaps. Shoot his toes off. Please, Crain, let me at him."

"Look, Jennifer, I know you want to do that," Crain said. "I don't really blame you. He probably deserves it.

Oh, what the hell. Go get him if you want him that badly."

Barton was frantic. "Crain, don't let that crazy woman back here. I'll talk to you, nobody else. How 'bout it, Crain. We got a deal?"

Brittin Crain moved back toward Barton's cell. "I don't know about the deal part, Barton. Looks to me like you're not in much of a position to be dealing anything. My hunch is you'd better start talking or this woman with this real big automatic is going to come back here and do some extensive remodeling on your one and only body."

"You people are crazy, Crain. You know that?"

"Yeah, I do," Crain replied. He laughed. "That's what makes us so dangerous. I'm listening."

Barton was so nervous he could hardly speak. He trembled while he gripped the bars. "I don't know what you want me to tell you, man. Where do I start?"

"Don't make a deal with that scum," Jill yelled. She was overplaying the role of the angry, distraught woman. "I want to kill that slime."

Crain turned quickly and faced Jill. "No, hold on just a minute, Jennifer. Even scum deserves a chance to justify himself. Let's hear what the man has to say. What say?"

"One minute, Crain. One minute, and if I don't like the sound of his voice, I get a shot at him. One kneecap. Agreed?"

"Agreed," Crain said. He turned back and faced Barton. "What about it, Barton?"

"I don't know, man. I said I would talk to you. I didn't say nothin' about havin' this crazy woman here."

"Okay, suit yourself," Crain said. He turned to walk away. "He's all yours, Jennifer."

Jill moved quickly to the front of the cell. She stopped abruptly and dropped into a crouch. She held a large automatic pistol in her hands. She aimed the weapon through the bars at Barton's legs. "You bastard!" she screamed. "You killed the man I loved. Bastard!"

"No," Barton screamed. "I was following orders. We all were. Miles did it. He set it all up. Please, no!"

The walkway and cell block roared with the concussion of gunfire.

Barton screamed, pleaded. Then he fell to the floor begging for mercy, but the gunfire roared again.

Chapter Eleven

"Something crazy is going on down there, boss" De-Witt said when Zave Auxton crawled up beside him. "Two big guys, one white and the other black, just arrived in that eighteen-wheeler. They stomped one of Miles's goons right there on the steps. Damnedest thing you ever saw. I thought it might break loose, but nobody bothered them after that. Something ain't exactly right down there."

"Okay," Auxton said. He sat upright and looked through his rubber-armored binoculars. "Sit tight and see what happens. I don't want us to make our move until the numbers thin. If they're all armed, and I'm sure they are, they got us outgunned ten or twelve to one. That isn't my kind of operating odds."

"Miles must be bringing the truckers in. I think something is going down soon. Real soon," DeWitt said.

"Did you recognize the two men who came in the truck?" Auxton asked.

"Never seen them before. From the looks of the greeting, whoever they are, somebody down there doesn't like them. You really think we can pull this thing off without blowing it?"

"I sure hope we can," Auxton said softly. "If we blow it, we'd better all hope we die. It'd be the lesser of two evils. Courts aren't too fond of cops who break the rules."

"Is everybody geared and ready?" DeWitt asked.

"Yeah. Maybe a little nervous, but ready. They want Miles just like we do and it doesn't matter what it takes."

"I'm not hearing much conversation down there. I can't get a handle on what they're up to yet, but I will," DeWitt said.

"Okay," Auxton replied. "Keep your eyes and ears working. If the situation changes or those people move out, let me know. We'll move just as soon as things clear out."

Carl hit the door and it opened with a loud thud. The glass panel vibrated, but didn't break. Carl hit the floor, rolling. The large black muzzle of the Uzi swept the interior of the steamy room for any potential threat. All it found was Miles, arm draped around the topless blonde, and a man with a clipboard standing beside the hot tub.

"What the hell is the meaning of this, boy?" Miles yelled.

"The *meaning* of this is, it's your turn to answer questions." Marc said. He stepped through another glass door on the opposite side of the room. He moved forward, the muzzle of his Uzi pointed directly at Miles's head.

Miles took his arm off the blonde. His face paled and he looked very afraid. "Ah was just gettin' ready to send ole Todd here to get in touch with you boys. Now what in tarnation are you comin' in here invadin' mah privacy like this for?"

"We don't like getting shot at," Carl said. "Suppose you tell us about a couple of your hardheads. Two guys. Barton and Dugan. They work on your docks. Of course, you should know that. Seems they didn't like us for one reason or another. They took a few of their best shots and they failed."

"What?" Miles said. "What on earth are you tellin' me?"

"Don't play dumb," Carl said. "Now, we came to you

lookin' for work. Whatever you had available. But if this is how you operate, our first job just might be a freebie. And you just might be it. Get the message?"

"I guess you're going to say you don't know anything about it. Am I right?" Marc asked.

"Ah sure as the devil don't," Miles said. "Where are them boys now?"

"They're no longer among us," Carl said. "When you play with fire, you'd best know how hot the flames can get. Barton and Dugan apparently didn't know that. Do you?"

"Ah swear it, I was sendin' for you. Tell 'em, Todd," Miles bellowed.

Todd was too scared to speak. He stood beside the hot tub shaking. It took a moment, but he finally found courage to force the words from his mouth. "He's telling the truth. I was just in here briefing Mr. Miles on your backgrounds. That is, I'm assuming you're Marc Lee and Carl Browne."

"You assumed right," Marc said. "How did you get any information on our backgrounds? That's military information. Nobody except government people have access to that."

"What do you think, bro, waste these pitiful excuses for humanity here and now and be done with it?" Carl asked. He kept the muzzle of his Uzi directed at Miles.

"We still don't have a job," Marc said.

"Hell with it," Carl said. His face grew tight and he bit down hard on his lips. His display of disgust was very convincing. "There's enough junk in this house we could steal and make enough money to carry us over until we can find something on the road. I don't trust this man. Not after what happened."

"Now, hold it just a minute, men," Miles pleaded. "You want a job, ole Bubba Ray can give you a job. Ah got a couple runs that could use men with your talents. Don't get too itchy with them trigger fingers."

"What kind of run?" Marc asked.

"A special kind. One with a cargo worth more money than you boys ever seen. The pay is a pretty nice piece of change, too. What say?"

"I'm not convinced," Carl bellowed. "You're just spouting off at the mouth. You're too vague. Talk names, numbers, and places. We'll decide if we're interested."

"All right," Miles said. "Ah got a run to Detroit and one to Flawda. They're both at the same time. You boys, uh, men, can have them. Both of them."

"We work as a team," Marc said coldly.

"Yeah, well, maybe you do," Miles said. "But these heah runs are special. That's double the money in the same amount of time. Mah trucks and mah cargo. A couple quick runs and a hell of a lot of quick spendin' money."

"What's the cargo?" Marc asked.

Miles hesitated, turned another shade whiter, and took a deep breath. "Quaaludes and methylamphetamines. Truck loads of 'em."

"What's the pay?" Carl asked.

"Uh, how's five grand apiece?"

"What are the shipments worth?" Marc asked.

Miles hesitated again. "Well, let me see. I'd say 'bout five or six million on the street."

"Five or six million?" Carl screamed. "And you offer us five thou each to be your mules? No way. Let's waste him, bro."

"Wait!" Miles screamed. "What's your price?"

"A hundred fifty thou each," Marc said sharply. "Half when we leave and half when we get back with the goods."

Miles almost lost his breath. "That there is sorta steep."

"Not as steep as losing five or six million if the goods never get here," Marc said.

"What?" Miles asked.

Carl almost laughed, but he kept a straight face. "If you

don't want to pay us to see that your junk gets here safely, then we could always see that it never does. It's up to you."

"You wouldn't," Miles mumbled.

"We came in here and got you, didn't we?" Carl asked. 'Now if we can do that, do you honestly think you could stop us on the highway if we really wanted to steal your junk?"

"Besides," Marc said, "you still haven't satisfied me on those two thugs that tried to kill us. I'm not a very happy man about that."

Miles contemplated an answer for a long moment. "Ah'll give you a hundred grand apiece."

"Waste 'em," Carl shouted. He lifted the muzzle of the subgun and his face was chiseled mean.

"All right! All right!" Miles screamed. "You got yo' price."

"Good," Marc said. "Now there is one more small detail."

"What's that?" Miles asked.

"We have any more problems out of your hardheads and we're coming to you. Next time, we shoot first and save the questions for later. Is that clear?"

"Todd, see that these men don't have no more problems from mah other people. Anybody," Miles said.

"Yes, sir," Todd replied. "I'll make sure the word is passed on to the men. I'll see to it personally."

"See that you do," Carl said. He spat fire into Todd's eyes. "Something goes wrong, when we come for Miles, we'll give you a dose of our special brand of medicine, too."

"Yes, sir," Todd said.

"When are these runs?" Marc asked.

"Whenever you're ready to go," Miles said. "Do we have a deal?"

"When you put long green cash in our hands," Carl said, "then you got a deal."

"Good," Miles said. "Ah'll have yo' cash just as soon a ah get all dried off."

"You're wasting our time," Marc said. He motione with the barrel of the Uzi in a gesture for Miles to get ou of the hot tub.

The blonde didn't move as Miles climbed slowly fron the steamy water. He looked at Marc and then Carl. "Yo boys really did kill your commandin' officer, didn't you?"

"That's right," Carl said coldly. "He was a jerk. W don't have much tolerance for jerks. He tried to screw us Set us up. You'd do well to remember that."

"Now, boys, don't go gettin' all excited," Miles said He dried himself slowly with a large towel, then wrapped i around his waist. "You treat Bubba Ray right and Bubb Ray will treat you right. Ahm a fair and honest man."

"Yeah, I can tell that by the quality of some of you employees. Your hired hands keep the kind of attitude the have now and you're gonna have a manpower shortage ver quickly," Marc said.

"Well," Miles said. "Some of mah boys just get a lathered up sometimes. They'll get used to you. Give 'em chance."

"Hey," Carl said. "We already gave 'em a chance. W didn't start the shooting or the fistfight, they did. It woulc probably be to your advantage to get the word out before more of them become shark meat. You catch my drift?"

Miles shot a hard glance at Carl. His eyes burned fire, but he obeyed his better judgment and kept his mouth shut.

Marc motioned with the gun barrel again. "Let's ge with the program. I'm a man of little patience, and right now, this place is getting on my one nerve."

"One more thing before we leave this room," Carl said. He knew it was time to bluff. "On our way in we placed ar explosive charge with a radio receiver detonator. Either one of us goes down and the other one makes it go boom

Just a little advice in case you have some cute tricks up your sleeve. If you do, I suggest you leave them there permanently. Any questions?"

"You boys really are hard and mean, ain't you?" Miles asked. He walked toward the glass door that led back into the main portion of the house.

"Harder and meaner than anybody you ever dealt with before," Marc said. His facial muscles tightened and he clenched his teeth. He shoved the Uzi forward in a deadly gesture.

"Yeah, well, ah can see that," Miles said. He picked up a robe near the door and put it on. "Follow me. We can get to mah private office and talk some business. Todd, you can come with us. You'll have to know the routes so's we can get the proper manifests issued to satisfy the ICC."

"Manifests for both routes, sir?" Todd asked.

"Yeah, both routes," Miles said. "We've got to get these trucks rollin'. When them eighteen-wheels ain't turnin', ah ain't makin' no money."

Miles led the way through the sprawling house. Marc and Carl followed. Both Warriors had their senses and skills on full alert, but there was no interference. They reached Miles's private office and Miles locked the door behind them.

"Awright," Miles said as he sat behind a large walnut desk in the center of the room. "You boys just go ahead and make yourselves comfortable. Now, there's two runs, like ah told you. Ah need one of you boys to go to Detroit with five of mah other rigs. The other one can go and make sure a delivery gets to Tallahassee, Flawda. These here jobs is real simplelike. Whoever goes to Detroit will pick up a shipment of mah goods and bring them back to Mobile. The run to Flawda is just as simple. You'll be goin' along with three other trucks. One is haulin' goods and the others is decoys. Whichever one of you goes on this run will be the only one that knows for sure which truck is haulin'. Of

course, the driver of the load will know he ain't runnin'
decoy. If they's any kind of trouble, you just call in on the
two-way. Now the federal boys and all them other narcotics
agents are keepin' a close eye on me and mah company. You
just might as well expect some trouble. Since ahm payin'
you boys such big, big money, ah expect these shipments to
get where it is they're goin'. If you need guns or ammani-
tion, ah got warehouses full of 'em. Tell me what it is you
want and you got it. With me payin' out this much cash, ah
expect the deliveries. No excuses."

Marc looked hard at Miles. "We'd like to inspect your
weapons stash and see just what you've got. We have high
expectations of our weapons and ammunition. We use only
the best. No cutting corners in that department."

"Awright," Miles said. "Ah'll have one of mah men,
Ronnie Richardson, take you to mah gun storage building.
Take whatever you want and forget you ever saw any of
it. Is that clear?"

"Clear," Marc said. "I wouldn't want it any other way."

"Good," Miles said. "We gonna get along just real
fine. Ah can tell this is gonna be a real good relationship
here." Miles looked up at Todd and nodded. "Todd, go to
the vault and get me a hundred and fifty thousand-dollars in
bundles. Get large bill bundles so they ain't so bulky."

"Yes, sir," Todd said obediently. "Be right back."

"Not that we don't trust you, you understand," Carl
said, "but I'll go with him. I'm still not convinced you didn't
know anything about the hit at the truckstop."

"He's right," Marc said. "You can hire our services, but
you've got to earn our trust. Until then, we're going to do
everything we can to cover our backside. Nothing personal,
it's just good business."

"Do whatever you got to do," Miles said. "Take him
with you, Todd."

"Yes, sir," Todd replied. He left the room with Carl
two steps behind him.

Miles waited until the door shut to the office and then he looked at Marc. "Tell me something. How did you get hooked up with a black boy? You seem like a reasonable and intelligent white man."

Marc's face immediately turned hard. His voice was low and cold and filled with undeniable confidence. "I am reasonable and intelligent. And that *black boy*, as you call him, is more of a man than any dozen white men you've got working for you. He's smart and he's damned good at what he does. Maybe even the best there is. Skin color's got nothing to do with his abilities. On top of that, that black man is like a brother to me. He's saved my life more times than I care to count and he's never asked one damned thing in return. I respect him; he respects me. If you know what's good for you, you'd do well to do the same. The last thing you ever want to do is make Carl Browne mad, because if you do, it could very well be the last thing you ever do."

"Ah see," Miles said sheepishly. "Ah was just curious."

Todd and Carl returned sooner than Marc had expected. When they entered the office, Todd was carrying a bulging cloth sack. Carl remained two or three steps behind with the muzzle of the Uzi ready to breath hellfire and death.

"Well, boys," Bubba Ray said. "That didn't take too long, now, did it?"

Todd placed the sack on the desk in front of Bubba Ray. "One hundred and fifty thousand-dollar bundles, Mr. Miles."

"Thank you, Todd," Miles said. He leaned forward and grabbed the sack at the bottom and lifted it up. A large pile of money dropped onto the desk and spilled. "Awright, let's us count out seventy-five stacks apiece. Then I want you boys to go with Ronnie to the warehouse."

"What then?" Carl asked.

"Meet tomorrow morning at seven at Bayside Transportation. Be on time."

"Where is it?" Marc asked.

"Six blocks south of mah shipping company. It's one ah own that not many people know about. Three other trucks and drivers will be there. The run for Flawda will be loaded and ready. The trucks for Detroit will be empty and runnin' deadhead." Miles paused and he took a bold chance. "From here on out, boys, ah call all the shots. Ah know you're both tough and ah know you're mean, but don't try to cross ole Bubba Ray Miles. Anybody that ever has ain't here to tell nobody about it. And don't either of you *ever* forget that. Now get your money and get on with the job you're bein' paid to do."

Marc and Carl took the money and placed it back in the cloth sack. When they reached the door, Marc stopped and stared into Bubba Ray's evil eyes. "Remember what I told you. Don't try to screw us. It would be your last mistake."

"Ah'll remember that," Bubba Ray said, and he smiled. "Ah'll call Ronnie and have him meet you at the door. Ah take it, since you found your way in, you can find your own way out. Get mah goods delivered and there's a whole lot more money where that came from."

Neither Warrior spoke. Instead, they moved carefully out the door and closed it behind them. They worked their way out of the house, met Ronnie Richardson, and left.

Miles waited at his desk until Marc and Carl had disappeared behind the heavy brush at the front of his house. He turned and faced Todd. "Get five of our best men in here. Ah got a few things ah need to go over with them."

"Are you going to allow those men to keep that much money, Mr. Miles?" Todd asked.

"Not in this lifetime," Bubba Ray said. "Go get me them truckers outside."

"Yes, sir," Todd replied. He left immediately.

Miles stretched his arms, found another cigar in his desk drawer, and lit it. He puffed on it until Todd reappeared five minutes later. Five men, all hardened by the nature of their work, followed him.

Miles greeted them. "Men, take a seat. Now, listen to me and listen carefully because ah don't want to say this but once. Tomorrow morning, there will be two men, one white and the other a nigger, that'll meet you at Bayside Transportation. Make your runs as usual, and when you find the opportunity, ah want you to kill both of them. Ah don't want them boys to come back to Alabam. That's clear and simple. Now, anybody that messes up will have to answer to me personally. Everybody that gets the job done the way it's s'posed to be gets a five-thousand-dollar bonus. And since ah don't care much for the darker-complexed brethren, the one that kills the nigger gets a double bonus of ten thousand dollars. Can you handle it?"

The men sat expressionless. Then they nodded in unison.

"Good," Bubba Ray said. "I knew I could count on you boys." He looked over at Todd again. "Todd, go get these boys a five-hundred-dollar cash bonus and let 'em go get a whore or something tonight."

"Yes, sir," Todd said.

"Boys, go have yourselves a helluva night on old Bubba Ray. Just be at the docks at bayside at six-thirty sharp and get this job done."

The men stood and left Miles's office. Todd followed. Several minutes passed and he returned. He sat down in a chair beside Bubba Ray's desk. "That's a very big risk you're taking, Mr. Miles. Those men are no amateurs. I think they mean what they say. I think they'll kill you if the drivers fail to eliminate them."

Miles finished his cigar and snuffed it out in the ashtray on his desk. "All just a part of doin' business the Miles-family way, Todd. Mah family's done it for generations. It sorta comes natural to me. Lee and Browne are gonna learn the hard way that nobody comes pushin' his way into Bubba

Ray Miles's house. Nobody tells Bubba Ray what to do. Ah killed better than them my own self when ah was establishin' mah territory some years ago. Ain't no tough-guy truckers gonna come in heah and tell me how to take care of mah business. Ah promise you that before this here week is out, them tough boys are gonna be just as dead as them po-leese that stuck their noses into mah business down on the docks. Now have somebody get me mah car. Soons ah get dressed, ah want to go into town and check around on some things personally."

Chapter Twelve

Carl activated the HDTV cameras and waited for Ronnie Richardson to get out of his car before he shut the Leeco rig down. They were in west Mobile away from Mobile Bay at a small industrial warehouse complex. "Something doesn't smell too good to me," Carl said.

"You keep an eye on Richardson. I'll watch our backside in case Miles or his cohorts have a surprise waiting for us," Marc said.

Carl scanned the area visually and then activated the infrared imaging device concealed on the Leeco trailer. He watched the computer screen as the images swept across. "Nothing showing that seems to present a concern."

"Good," Marc said. "He's getting out."

"Okay, we're on. Let's go see what kind of toys Miles has in his toy closet," Carl said. He opened the cab door and shifted from the seat. When he was partially down the side of the cab, he glanced over his shoulder as a precaution to see where Richardson was.

Marc also climbed out. He slipped from the seat and grabbed the handrail. The first step sent pain crashing through him. He still hadn't recuperated from the severe beating earlier in the day. The pain slowed him, but he was determined it wouldn't stop him.

Marc reached the ground and looked around. It appeared clear, so he moved to the front of the long-nosed Leeco rig and met Carl. Richardson was already there.

"You're the tour guide," Carl said. "Show us the way."

"In here," Richardson said. "The back of the warehouse. Follow me."

Richardson unlocked a heavy steel door beside three overhead doors. He opened it and stepped inside. Then he stopped at a central station burglar alarm panel and entered a digital sequence to shut off the alarm. That done, he switched on rows of overhead lights at a switch box near the alarm panel. "Back this way," he said.

The Highway Warriors followed. So far, nothing was out of the ordinary. Neatly stacked rows of corrugated boxes lined the floors and walls. Neatly printed cardboard signs identified each row with a stock number. Then, twenty feet from the back wall, Richardson stopped beside a closed doorway that led into an area partitioned off with heavy concrete blocks and steel bars. The area, probably sixty-five feet square and forty feet high, resembled a large cage sitting in the middle of the floor. It rose upward and stopped less than three feet from the high ceiling. Steel reinforcement bracings half an inch thick and four inches wide extended horizontally along the outer concrete blocks like a giant belt enclosing the blocks. Carl looked at the steel carefully and figured it was either a false steel ceiling inside the partitioned area or additional supports for a second floor inside. Either way, it was strong and very durable.

"In we go, guys," Richardson said. "Bubba Ray must trust you two. Besides me, Todd, and Bubba Ray, no one knows of this storage facility. Before we go in, let me warn you. There is enough weaponry and ammunition inside here to start a major war. No one comes here much. Bubba Ray will occasionally come in and pick himself a toy to play with back at the farm. This place is very hush-hush. When we leave, it would be a good idea if both of you forgot you were ever here."

"Understood," Carl said.

Richardson unlocked a high-security internal lock and lifted the heavy steel door handle. The door swung open and exposed another steel door heavier than the first. Richardson worked an electronic combination and twisted the access lever. The door opened and lights came on automatically. "Here we are," he said, and gestured toward the room. "Bubba Ray's gun room."

Carl stepped in first and Marc followed. Their eyes widened when they saw the interior of the room.

"Impressive," Marc said.

"It should be," Richardson said. "It cost enough. You'll notice the air is a little dry. That's because the room is dehumidified. There is little or no moisture in the air. All outside air is filtered so there's no dust. The internal temperature is exactly controlled. There are no liquid-carrying pipes anywhere in the vicinity. All walls and floors are covered and sealed in heavy clear acrylic. The weapons are stored for long-term storage. Oiled, greased, that kind of thing. The room is divided into four parts. Two lower levels, two upper. Steel and concrete reinforce everything interior and exterior. As you can see, the assortment is almost endless."

"I'm impressed," Marc said. He looked at the rows of gun racks filled to capacity. There were Colt M-16s, AR-15s, H&K MP-5s, 92s, 93s, Uzis, Ingrams, fully automatic AK-47s, old Smith & Wesson subguns, Remington 870 riot guns, Mossberg 500 riot guns, Sako sniper rifles with attached high-power telescopic sights, and assorted World War II vintage military rifles.

"I think the man is armed for serious business," Carl said.

"This *is* a serious business, Mr. Browne," Richardson said. "One of the other rooms contains rocket launchers and grenades. Another is the ammunition room. Come on, I'll show you. You might start thinking about what your selections will be. Mr. Miles said you are authorized to take whatever you want."

"I'm starting to like him," Marc said. He looked at Richardson and saw that the guy was falling for his line. For the first time, he saw his tense muscles relax just a little.

"You named three rooms," Carl said. "What's in the fourth?"

"Explosive devices and a miscellaneous collection of detonators. Fuses, timers, and the like."

"This stuff didn't come from the local gun shop," Carl said. "Where did Miles get it?"

"That's something only he knows," Richardson said. "He's never said and no one has ever had the courage to ask. A new shipment just *appears* from time to time. You must understand, Mr. Miles is a man with many connections. He knows people in all the *right* places. He takes care of them and they take care of him. That's his business."

"Okay," Carl said. "What's next?"

"The ammunition room. This way," Richardson said.

He unlocked another steel door and another room became illuminated by bright lights. Inside, there was a mountain of ammunition that reached the ceiling. All of the sealed boxes, cans, and crates were labeled and cataloged by bullet type and caliber.

"Amazing," Marc said. "There must be at least a couple million rounds in here."

"Four million, to be exact," Richardson said, smiling. "Like I said earlier, there's enough in here to start a serious war."

"What about a fire?" Carl asked.

"No problem. The walls are twenty-two inches of steel-reinforced concrete and concrete blocks. It's almost like a bank vault. This entire building could burn to the

ground and this storage area would not only remain standing, it would be completely unharmed on the inside.
Heating, cooling, dehumidification, all air, comes through
shielded ducts in the floor. Everything is belowground.
The climate control instrumentation is in a building a
hundred yards behind this warehouse. That's an ample
distance for even the worst fire."

"Theft?" Marc asked.

"Not a problem," Richardson said. "You saw for yourself the extreme integrity of this structure. Nothing short of
a high-explosive missile could possibly penetrate it. The
alarm system is wired to the office of Miles Shipping and
Drydock. A second alarm sounds in Todd's office in the
basement at the farm. Understandably, we don't have a
need for police on something like this."

"What's in the explosive room?" Carl asked.

"C-four mostly. Also some dynamite and a few other
little things," Richardson said. "There's every kind of
detonator you can imagine. Must be dozens of different
things up there. It's on the second floor."

"Okay," Marc said. "I'd feel much better about this if
we could meet here at say six o'clock in the morning. I see
some things I'd like to take on the run, but we may be hot
since our run-in at the truckstop this morning. It might be
better if we don't take the wares now. Keeping them with
us overnight worries me. How about you, Carl?"

"I think that's the best way to handle it," Carl said.
"Any problem with that, Ronnie?"

"I don't see why there should be. I'll spend the night
in town and meet you here at six. Take what you need to
take care of Mr. Miles. You do good, and he'll see that
you're properly compensated. He may be a lot of things,
but I guarantee you he's a man of his word. It's a Miles-
family tradition. Their word is their bond. Always has
been."

"Okay, six o'clock it is," Marc said. "Let's finish our

walk-through and leave this place. All this heavy firepower is a load to take in all at once. Wow. It even makes *me* a little nervous."

Joe McNally didn't like to drive Bubba Ray Miles's car, but sometimes, like now, he found himself burdened with that responsibility. He drove the Cadillac along Route 43 south toward Mobile. Miles sat in the backseat and puffed on a large cigar. McNally occasionally glanced into the rearview mirror and verified what he already knew: Bubba Ray was in a very bad mood.

Todd had warned him that Miles had let go of a large amount of cash. Gave it to the truckers, Lee and Browne. And that, McNally knew, was something Bubba Ray Miles hardly ever did unless he expected to gain something well worth the price of his investment.

McNally looked into the mirror again. "Hey, Bubba Ray, we're almost in Mobile. Where are we going?"

"Take me to the docks. Ah got some business to take care of with the longshoremen," Miles said.

"Right," McNally said. He could tell by the sound of Bubba Ray's voice that the little wheels were turning inside his head. He knew Miles was up to something. Just what, he wasn't quite sure.

Zave Auxton crawled back through the dense under-brush and aimed his binoculars at Miles's house three hundred yards away. He could still see men moving erratically around the grounds. There had been some excitement earlier when one of the hired hands had found the gate guard gagged and bound in the underbrush. DeWitt had captured the excited conversation on tape through the parabolic listening device. But now that had settled and the blame fell on the two men in the eighteen-wheeler who had come to the house and since left.

"You think they've let their guard down enough to move?" DeWitt asked.

"I don't think so," Auxton replied.

"What are you thinking?" DeWitt asked.

"I know I said we'd stay until the job was done," Auxton said, "but Miles is gone. I think we need to pull back and assess what we already have. Those guys in the big truck threw a wrench in the system. I want to know who they are and where they came from."

"All appearances indicate they may not be total friend-lies with Miles and company," Dewitt said. "That guard and the incident on the steps tells me they're riding Miles for something. Personally, I'd like to know what it is."

"Me too," Auxton said. "Something's going on that we aren't aware of. I want more information before we move in."

"Miles is scrambling for something," DeWitt said. "He's either moving stuff in or out. And he's doing it in a big way. We need to know what we're walking into before we go in."

"Okay, it'll be dark in an hour and a half. We'll take it in shifts," Auxton said. "Two men each." He lowered the binoculars and rolled onto his side. "Get everything on tape and get as much film footage as we can. Use the infrared equipment tonight and monitor everything that goes on down there. Stay here twenty-four hours a day until it's time. We blew it once on the docks. We got our butts kicked and lost a lot of good men. That one was a bloodbath. Now we're going to hit him where he lives. Where it hurts. We won't blow it this time."

Thomas Barton knew he was dead. His ears were ringing from the massive concussion of the gunfire. He felt the pain. But then he realized it was old pain renewed. It occurred to him that he wasn't dead. He looked up from the floor where he cowered like a frightened child. The woman was still standing there. Her face was chiseled lean, but despite it she was very pretty. A large automatic pistol remained clutched in her hands. She was wearing hearing protectors and shooting glasses as if she were on a firing range for a leisurely afternoon of shooting. Barton knew something wasn't right, because the woman appeared competent with the big gun. So, he wondered, how had she missed him?

Barton kept his left arm draped across his face in a pathetic attempt to shield himself from further gunfire. "You tried to kill me," he screamed.

The woman remained in her stone-carved position. "You should be so lucky. You're still alive, aren't you?"

"What?" Barton asked.

"You're still alive. If I'd *tried* to kill you, you'd be dead."

"Who are you?"

"For what it matters to you, I'm Jennifer Lane."

"This is murder," Barton pleaded.

"Oh no, not yet," Jill said coldly. "The first two were blanks just to get your attention. I'll give you some advice. The next fourteen aren't. I'd like to just go ahead and blow your sorry brains out, but in all fairness I guess I should give you a chance. That's more than you and Miles's filth gave those cops on the docks. Do you want to reconsider your position about talking to us?"

Barton tightened himself into a ball. "What do you want me to say? I just work on the docks. I don't know everything that goes on there."

"You know enough."

"So what? What is it you want from me?"

"You're wasting my time," Jill chided. She raised the big automatic to point shoulder and leveled it on Barton's head.

"Okay! Okay!" Barton screamed. "I'll tell you everything I know."

"Good boy," Jill said. "Crain, come in here."

The large metal door slammed again and Crain moved along the walkway. "Yeah," he said.

"Mr. Barton has decided to continue his conversation with us," Jill said.

"Mighty nice of him," Crain said.

Jill stared into Barton's frightened eyes. "What do you know about the bloodbath on Miles's docks?"

Barton hesitated, his arm still perched in front of his face. "What do you want to know?"

"Were you there?" Jill asked.

"Yes."

"Don't keep me in suspense. I'm a very impatient woman. What happened?" Jill asked harshly.

"Miles set the whole thing up. He knew that Baxter guy was a narc. He knew he was wired, too. He figured he could lure the agents in and kill all of them."

"And he expected that to keep the heat off of his operation for a while?" Crain asked.

"Yeah, kinda. He knew that would make the cops mad and maybe even scare 'em a little. He figured they couldn't put him there personally, so he was clear. That would give him time to make other arrangements for his drug distribution. But then the plan went to hell when that guy, Filbert I think was his name, with the street dealer recognized Baxter. It blew up before Miles was ready. He was really ticked off about that, too, man. I mean he was really mad."

"So then what?" Crain asked.

"When the cops heard their man on the inside was in trouble, they hit. We were waiting for them, but not that soon."

"Who is 'we'?"

"About twenty of us longshoremen. We work the docks with Miles's shipments. They're all a tough bunch of guys. They don' take no crap. You know what I'm talking about?"

"Yeah, I know," Crain said. "Did you ambush the police officers on the dock that night?"

"Yeah, it was kinda funny. They come bustin' in doors and walls and everything. They didn't see nobody on the docks, so they thought it was all clear. We let 'em get into the open and then we started cuttin' 'em down. They never had much of a chance to know what hit 'em."

"I see," Crain said. "And the van. The listening post out on the street in front of the building. What happened there?"

"A couple of guys got a big front-end loader and lifted it up. They hauled it to the dock and dumped it into the bay. Drowned the guys inside."

"What did Miles do then?"

"He panicked. I mean, man, he was scared shitless. He got out. Two of us were behind him when he went across the roof with Ronnie Richardson and Joe McNally. There was a cop up there, and Bubba Ray killed him. Walked up to him and stuck a gun in his face and pulled the trigger. I don't think he knew we was behind him. If he had, he might have killed us, too. He's got a thing about witnesses when he does something bizarre."

"You saw him shoot the cop?"

"Yes."

"Did you see him kill anybody else?"

"No, it was too dark everywhere else. Only reason I could see the roof was because there was one of them mercury-vapor dock lights high on a pole. It lit the top of the roof enough for me to see. Scared the hell outta me." Barton removed his arm and let it drop to his side. He seemed to relax a little, as if he felt relieved.

"Okay, what happened at the docks this morning?" Crain asked.

"Two real mean guys, one white and one black, came in sayin' they was lookin' for work. Said they wanted to see Bubba Ray. We got into a fistfight and they beat the tar out of about ten or twelve guys. Pissed everybody off, so we drew straws to see who would go kill them when they left. Me and Billy Dugan drew the short straw. I guess we really got the short end of the stick in more ways than one, huh?"

"Yes, I'd say you did," Crain replied.

Barton talked for an hour. He told everything he could remember. He designated three other locations were Miles warehoused drugs or other contraband. Fatigue was showing on his face when he finally looked Crain in the eyes. "I don't know anything else to tell you."

"One more question," Crain said. "Where does Miles get his local information?"

"Like what?"

"Like how did he know what the police were doing? How did he know about Baxter?" Crain asked.

"Bubba Ray Miles got eyes and ears all over the place. He can find out anything," Barton said.

"He has someone inside Mobile PD?" Jill asked.

"Yeah, sure."

"Do you know who his source is?" Jill asked. She felt her blood pressure rising and her breathing changed. She held on, suspended in time, waiting for Barton's reply.

Brittin Crain jerked his head up, his attention piqued. "Well?" he said.

"Yes, I know. Hell, I think everybody around there knows. Miles has been padding this clown for a long, long time. He gives huge amounts of money for information and it comes in regular as clockwork. He needs something special, any of us do, we just pick up the telephone." Barton paused and then laughed. "You know, dial a dirty cop. Simple as that."

Chapter Thirteen

"Surfsider, this is Pathfinder. Do you copy? Over."
Marc released the talk switch and let the Icom microphone
drop to his lap.

"Must be busy with our boy Barton," Carl quipped.
"I'll bet he's singing like a canary."

"I'll try him again," Marc said. He lifted the microphone. "Surfsider, this is Pathfinder. Over."

"Roger, Pathfinder. This is Surfsider," Jill's voice said
over the Icom speaker. "Do you have traffic?"

"Roger, Surfsider. We need to meet. Over."

"Affirmative, Pathfinder. We have new information on
this end," Jill said.

"Same here," Marc replied. "Where's Brittin?"

"He's finishing some conversation with your gift package."

"Roger. Where do you want to make the meet?"

"Stand by. I'll get back with you in a few minutes. I
need to talk with Brittin," Jill said.

"Roger. Where's Harrison?" Marc asked.

"He's following up on some new leads. We have
several things here we need to update you on. How long
before you could meet?"

"Name it. We're leaving the west side of town now.

147

We're on Cottage Hill Road. We're going to roll south in a minute and get toward the interstate highway. We could be anywhere in the vicinity you want us to be in, say, thirty to forty-five minutes."

"Roger," Jill said. "Give me five minutes and I'll have the info for you."

"Roger, Pathfinder standing by."

"Surfsider clear."

Marc slid the microphone back into the mike bracket and looked over at Carl. "Wonder what they've got."

"I imagine Barton spilled his guts. If we can sort all of this out, maybe we can bring Miles and company down in the next forty-eight hours. What do you think?"

Marc contemplated his answer for a few seconds. "I think our run tomorrow with Miles's eighteen-wheelers will tell us everything. I don't think Miles will stand idly by and let us know any more than we already do about his operation. On top of that, I certainly don't think he's going to let us get very far with a hundred and fifty thousand of his money. He's too shrewd and too greedy for that."

"Agreed," Carl said. He rolled the big Leeco machine along Government Boulevard. A sign ahead indicated the entry ramp for Interstate 65 south. He got into the right lane and signaled. "What do you think he'll try to do to stop us?"

"Oh, no doubt about it, he'll try a hit. Could come before the run or it could come during the run. He'll have us divided. The oldest theory in the book. Divide and conquer. But once we get to his weapon stash in the morning, I have a plan."

The Icom speaker crackled with Brittin Crain's voice. "Pathfinder, this is Surfsider. Are you out there, guys?"

Marc lifted the noise canceling microphone and spoke. "Roger, old man. Go ahead."

"The lady says you want a meet. I think that would be

a very good idea. We've got much to talk about. Over," Crain said.

"Affirmative, Surfsider. How about Fort Conde in thirty minutes? Over."

"Fort Conde it is," Crain replied. "Anything else pressing before we go?"

"Negative, nothing else pressing," Marc replied. "See you in thirty minutes."

"Wonder what he's got going?" Carl asked. He reached the end of the southbound entry ramp, checked in his mirrors and over his left shoulder for traffic, and then grabbed another gear to move onto the interstate highway.

"Hard to say," Marc said.

"Could be Barton knew more than he was willing to talk about at first. He wasn't feeling any too good when I held court with him," Carl said. He moved the big Leeco rig into the left lane to merge into Interstate 10 eastbound.

"One thing still bothers me," Marc said. "Miles must have a very reliable source high on the inside of the official political structure somewhere. Could be the police department, but it doesn't necessarily have to be. Could be all of our efforts and Crain's have focused on the forest and missed the trees."

"We can speculate until we turn green," Carl said. He moved into the right lane and slowed the rig slightly. "Maybe Brittin will have something to enlighten us."

"Yeah," Marc said. "We'll know in a little while, won't we?"

Brittin Crain was sitting in a beige Dodge when Carl stopped the rig at Fort Conde. Jill was in the front passenger seat. Benjamin Jasper and Dianne Oakley were in the backseat. Both were very nervous.

When the cab doors opened on the big Leeco rig, Crain got out of the car. Jill, Jasper, and Oakley followed.

"Hey, bro," Carl said when he shook hands with Crain. The handshake was more out of friendship than protocol. "Who are your guests?"

"It's a long story," Brittin said. He turned and faced Jasper and Oakley. "This is Detective Dianne Oakley and Detective Benjamin Jasper. They're Mobile PD. Dianne was engaged to one of the men killed on the docks. They're clean, just in case you're worried. How are you feeling, Marc?"

"Like I've been run over by a truck," Marc replied. He wrapped his arms around Jill and gave her a solid hug. "What's new?"

"We've located more of Miles's storerooms," Crain said. "Barton sang big time. Although I have to admit, it might not have been complete willingness on his part. Jill managed a bit of not-so-subtle persuasion."

"He's leaving the best part out," Jill said. "We know how Miles's network operates and where he makes his major runs. We also have information that could tell us who the leak is on the inside. Barton swears to it and Harrison is running down the information as we speak. When he has verification, we can make a takedown."

"Why don't we go inside the rig and get comfortable. Carl and I have something we need to share with you also." Marc said.

"Sounds like a good idea," Crain said.

"Inside?" Jasper asked, puzzled.

"Inside," Carl replied.

Jasper looked at Oakley and they exchanged bewildered stares.

The group walked to the rear of the Leeco trailer and Carl activated the digital code to open the doors. They entered, got comfortable in the living quarters, and spent the next hour and a half assembling the puzzle pieces to Bubba Ray Miles's criminal empire.

Finally, Carl stood and stretched. "Anything else?"

"That about covers it," Crain said. "Time is running short. Let's rock-and-roll."

Marc crawled through the darkness toward Miles's warehouse on Pleasant Street. A preliminary scan by the infrared imaging equipment of the building and the area surrounding it showed only one sentry posted haphazardly in a makeshift guard post near the front of the warehouse. Marc paused, checked his Icom U-16 transceiver on his belt, and switched on the VOX switch box. He spoke softly, just loud enough to activate the VOX circuitry for the transmitter. "I'm almost in position on this side, Major. How goes it over there?"

"Give me thirty seconds on this side," Carl said. "I've got a mercury-vapor light to deal with over here. You see anything else?"

"Negative," Marc replied. "Just the one guy. He looks old. Not Miles's type. He could be a security guard for the entire complex. I think a little induced sleep would do him good."

"Affirmative. When you're in position, I'll make a little distraction out here to flush him out of his post. When he comes out, he's yours."

"Roger," Marc said. His BDUs slid effortlessly over the grass-covered ground toward the guard's window. His all-black clothing made him blend into the darkness, become a part of it. He carried his silenced Uzi on its sling over his back beside a large black backpack. Extra magazines and detonators filled his musette bag, riding low on his right hip. The black backpack was filled with Delta Force Composition-2. The experimental high explosive possessed unique stability and exceptional ignition capability. Although it had not been cleared for current Delta Force issue, General A.J. Rogers at Delta Force Command in Washington had seen fit to supply a large quantity to the Highway Warriors for use in the never-ending war on American crime. In field trial, DFC-2 had proven superior to current-issue Composition-4. And soon, it would encounter another series of tests.

"I'm in position," Carl said. "You call it."

"Roger," Marc said. "I'm going silent for a minute or so until I can get right where I want to be. I'll give you the call to make the distraction. When he comes out, I'll handle it."

"Roger. Waiting on your command," Carl said.

Marc slid a dart gun from the musette bag and lifted it until he could see the breech of the bolt-action weapon. He opened the bolt and lifted a syringelike dart from the musette bag. He slid it into the breech and closed the bolt. He double-checked the action and the safety then crawled toward the edge of the metal warehouse where the guard sat at a desk. After he had secured himself behind the edge of the building, he brought the dart gun up to point shoulder and held it steady. "Now!" he said into the VOX microphone.

A loud crash rumbled across the front of the building. Carl had kicked a large fifty-five-gallon barrel onto its side and sent it rolling across the lot. The empty barrel roared louder than a thunderclap and reverberated around the big building. Carl ducked back to cover and held steady.

The guard's door burst open and he came out like a charging legionnaire. He held a MagLite flashlite in one hand and .38 Special revolver in the other.

Marc watched. The guy moved forward, the muzzle of the revolver searching shakily for something in the darkness. He shone the broad beam of the flashlight around the area, craning his neck to see. He moved the light in a predictable pattern along the base of the high chain-link fence that surrounded the front of the warehouse. Then the light jerked to a stop. The guard moved it back to his right and stopped again. The beam shone upon a pair of beady eyes reflecting back from the darkness. A cat.

Marc steadied his aim and snapped off the shot. A pop preceded a whoosh. The sound of the dart impacting the guard's shoulder was a dull thud.

The guard reached backward, clutching for the dart, but his efforts were futile. His knees buckled and he collapsed to the pavement.

"Clear," Marc said. "Let's do it."

"Movin'," Carl replied. He came up from his knees and ran hard along the leading edge of the building. He met Marc at the guard shack.

Marc held the guard by the armpits. When Carl opened the door, he slid the sleeping man inside and put him back in his chair. He folded the guy's arms on the desk and placed his head on it gently. Then he removed the dart from the guard's back and slipped it inside a plastic protective sleeve. He slid the missile back into his musette bag.

"He'll wake up and wonder why he went to sleep," Marc said. "He may have a little touch of a headache tomorrow, but he won't remember a thing."

Carl glanced at his watch. "Let's hump it. Time's wastin'."

Marc took the keys from the guard's key ring and sorted through them until he found one that fit the door to the warehouse. He opened the door and ducked inside.

Carl followed.

They found the breaker box for the overhead lighting and switched the lights on.

Marc looked at his wristwatch. "You take the front and the south side. I'll do the rear and the north side. Ten minutes and we're out of here. Deal?"

"Deal," Carl said. He broke into a run toward the south wall of the giant warehouse.

Marc moved to the north wall. He immediately slipped the backpack from his back and opened it. He removed pliable bricks of the off-white DFC-2 and unwrapped them from their waxed paper. He placed the first one against the I-beam steel supports and pressed it into shape. Then he removed a small detonator-receiver from his musette bag and pressed it into the DFC-2 compound. He flipped a small DIP switch on the top of the detonator-receiver and waited for the arming chirp.

It came.

Marc made his way along the wall of the warehouse. He placed a charge every thirty feet until he had covered both walls. Then he glanced at his watch. Three minutes to go. He spoke into the VOX headset. "How's it going, Major?"

"I got one more to do and I'm out of here," Carl said.

"Good. I'm going outside to set up the receiver and minitransmitter."

"Go for it!" Carl replied.

Marc ran for the door. He opened it carefully to be sure the guard was undisturbed. One glance into the room revealed the man sleeping in the same position he had left him. Marc walked past him to the outer door. He checked the area around the warehouse, but nothing had changed. He worked his way back along the side of the building toward the high weeds and brush in a nearby vacant lot. He crept lightly to a utility pole with a ground-level switching box mounted on it. He reached into the backpack, found one of three microtransceivers there, brought it out, and set it on the box. He removed the cover from the microtransceiver and punched a sequence of numbers into the keypad; the digits on the LCD display indicated the receiver's operating frequency. Satisfied, Marc pressed "Enter." The receiver beeped. Marc then programmed in the microtransmitter frequency and pressed "Enter" again.

He set the tiny unit on the ground and rummaged for the portable turnstile antenna inside the backpack. He found it, unfolded it, and attached the coaxial connector to the microtransceiver. Then he moved the entire unit beneath the switching box and covered it in loose dead grass and weeds.

"I'm on-line out here, Major. You out of there yet?"

"Yeah, Colonel, I'm out. What about the keys?"

"I put them back on the guard's key chain before I left."

"Roger. Lights are off, doors shut and locked, guard's still sawing logs. Are we out of here?"

"We're out," Marc replied. "See you at the Jeep."

"Got it," Carl said. "Damn shame we can't be here to see this one."

"Hey, we can't be everywhere at once," Marc replied. "But the bird can." He worked his way back through the darkness toward the custom Jeep Cherokee. When he got there, Carl was waiting.

"Well, bro, one down and one to go," Carl said.

"Yeah, Pleasant Street isn't going to be so pleasant come morning."

"I got to hand it to you, this is one of your better plans. I would never have thought of it. Tell me one more time how those things work," Carl said. He fired the Jeep and dropped it into gear.

"Simple really," Marc said. "At exactly six minutes and twenty-three seconds after eight o'clock in the morning, the Russian weather satellite Meteor two-nine will come into target range over the horizon. It constantly transmits a signal in the selected one hundred and thirty-seven megahertz range. When the microreceiver receives that circular polarized signal through the turnstile antenna, it will trigger the microtransmitter, which in turn transmits a tone signal to all of the receiver-detonators placed in the DFC-two material. Then it's bye-bye baby. Everything goes boom and we're nowhere near the place. All of the devices will self-destruct and the only thing remaining of the warehouse, any drugs there, and the devices, will be tiny chunks of trash and ash."

"Why the Russian satellite?" Carl asked. He steered the Jeep along Pleasant Street and stared through the windshield into the darkness.

Marc smiled as he arranged a new supply of explosives inside his backpack. "I used the computerized tracking program in the computer on the rig. It tracks and calculates a target range for polar-orbiting satellites. That tells you precisely when the bird will peep over the horizon and the signal can be received with a simple turnstile antenna and microreceiver. It combines the rotation of the earth and the orbit schedule of the satellite. Meteor two-nine is the only satellite that will make a pass at a time that could be used to our advantage in the morning. Satellites are constantly passing overhead. Their orbits can be tracked and predicted to within a tenth of a degree longitude and latitude by using the resources we have available in the rig. Nothing else anywhere near is on their particular frequency, so there's no chance of a stray detonation. We could have used any of several satellites, but the Russian bird just happened to be the one that fit the bill."

"I like it," Carl said. "The Russians are gonna invade Mobile, blow all hell out of that place, put a serious dent in Bubba Ray Miles's empire, and no one will ever know how. Clever."

"Thanks," Marc said. "We could have accomplished the same thing utilizing the ComSat-D system, but that would require a manual detonation. Knowing Miles, anything could happen between now and the time we want to blow the place. This way, if something should go sour in the morning, it won't make any difference. This one goes automatically."

Carl drove through the night until they were two blocks from Miles Shipping and Drydock Company. He parked the Jeep Cherokee in a deserted building lot and shut it down. "Same game, Colonel?" he asked.

"This one might be a little more volatile than the last one," Marc said. "I figure Miles keeps people here twenty-four hours a day. We're going to have to wing it. Do you have a good overview of the maps Jasper and Oakley provided?"

"Yeah," Carl said. "I got it. This place is broken into so many different buildings, we're going to have to move fast."

"Okay," Marc said. "Same game. You take the front and south and I'll take the rear and the north. Fifteen minutes and we're out of here. If you aren't finished by then, leave with what you've gotten done. Try to avoid any contact with the longshoremen. We end up leaving somebody down and they're going to know something's amiss."

"Affirmative," Carl said. "You ready?"

"Ready," Marc replied. "Let's wire this one for some bayside fireworks."

The Warriors climbed from the Jeep, secured it, and moved into the dark shadows along the docks on Mobile Bay. They reached the first building in the Miles complex on the south end of the dock.

"Stay together until we get inside, then we split up," Marc said.

Carl nodded and followed Marc's lead. They entered through a broken window and made their way to the center of the dirty, musty building. Marc looked at Carl in the ambient glow from the dockside lights and nodded his head. Carl acknowledged and they split up.

Carl went directly to the front walls and repeated the procedure used at Pleasant Street. He placed DFC-2

charges and inserted receiver-detonators. He worked fe-
verishly, checking his watch every few minutes to be sure
he was on schedule.

Marc also worked frantically. He climbed over boxes
and crates until he could reach the support structure of the
building. There had been no sign of intervention from any
of Miles's longshoremen. Marc had one charge remaining.
He looked at his watch. Two minutes and fifteen seconds
until it was time to clear the area. He grabbed the charge
and placed it near the electrical box in the corner at the
back of the building. The docks were covered and so were
all of the buildings now. Marc set up the microtransceiver
and the turnstile antenna. Another glance at his watch
showed one minute and five seconds. He climbed from the
crates and worked his way back to the center of the first
building where he had left Carl. When he got there, Carl
was waiting.

"All done, Colonel," Carl said.

"Same here. Let's book out of this place."

The Warriors moved toward the broken window at
dockside, careful to avoid contact with anything that would
make noise. They reached the window and checked the
dock. It was clear. There was no sign of Miles's longshoremen.

Carl looked at Marc and grinned. "We did it, Colonel."

Lights suddenly came on from every direction. The
darkened warehouse lit up to the intensity of daylight.
The Warriors spun in unison, fisting their silenced Uzis in
the process. Lights blinded them, but as they shielded
their eyes from the intense beams they could see a dozen
gun barrels pointed at their faces.

A deep, gruff Southern-accented voice growled, "Ah
sorta suspected you boys would do something stupid like
try to break in heah and steal mah drugs. You didn't fool ole
Bubba Ray for one minute, nosirree. Ain't no drugs heah,

though. You boys just don't seem to recanize who you're dealin' with. Remember what ah told you: 'Don't try to screw old Bubba Ray.' Now ahm gonna get mah money's worth and teach you boys a real hard-learned lesson . . . Miles Southern style."

Chapter Fourteen

□ □ □

Zave Auxton scanned the perimeter of Bubba Ray Miles's house through the night-vision scope. He looked away from the telescope and directly at DeWitt. "Okay, my man, it's time!"

"Right," DeWitt said. "I'll disassemble everything and load it in the Blazer. Give me five minutes, ten tops, and I'll be ready to go."

"Get with it," Auxton said. "I'll tell the others. As soon as everything is checked and rechecked, we'll move out."

DeWitt started the disassembly process for the electronic surveillance equipment. He removed the large camera and lens from the tripod, stripped them into individual components, and packed them in heavily padded nylon cases. Each case was labeled with large white letters: Mobile Police Department. When the camera was secure, he removed the microphone from the boom element on the parabolic listening device. He folded the dish reflector until it resembled a small hand fan like the ones that were once so prominent in the Old South. Then he packed the tape recorders and video cameras into separate padded nylon carrying cases. When it was all finished, he grabbed the handles of as many cases as he could carry and headed through the underbrush toward the Chevy Blazer.

Auxton had already joined the other men, Jim Kelly

and Mike Croft. They sat in a tight circle, flanked by an impressive assortment of assault weapons and night-vision devices. Everyone ran final weapons checks to verify function and the status of chambers and magazines.

Zave Auxton was relaxed, cool and calculating. He knew the drill, had memorized the plan, had run it through his mind a thousand times in his fantasies, but this time it was the real thing. This time it was deadly, but the plan was simple.

Jim Kelly finished his weapons check first. He looked over at Auxton, who was holstering a Beretta-92F 9mm automatic. "Boss, how do you stay so calm? Aren't you the least bit nervous?"

"Ain't no thing," Auxton said. "We're just going to rid this world of a little more garbage, that's all. This thing has gone too far. Miles has crossed way over the line. It's got to stop."

"What if there are more men inside that we don't know about?" Mike Croft asked.

"We handle it," Auxton said. "The simple equation for success. In fast and hard. No mistakes. No mercy. No survivors. No witnesses."

"Bubba Ray Miles is a shrewd operator," Kelly said. "I just have a tough time thinking he's got the security so lax that we can get in and get out without some surprises."

"If it makes you nervous, don't do it. If you can't give a hundred percent, say it now. Anybody. If you're feeling weak or you've just changed your mind, get up and walk away right now. Nobody is going to think less of you for it. I mean that. Anybody wants out, this is the time. Ten minutes from now you're in it for life."

Kelly and Croft sat still and remained silent.

"Okay," Auxton said. "As soon as DeWitt makes the last run to the truck, it's play time."

"Makin' it now, boss," DeWitt said as he passed by

with the second and last load of surveillance equipment for the truck.

"Okay," Auxton said. "Make one more check of your goodies. Let's do this right the first time, because there isn't going to be a second chance. Check the steel inserts in your vests. Get your straps snug, because there's a very good chance you're going to take some hits down there. They aren't going to let us come in and then walk out again without some fireworks."

"We wearing the goggles, boss?" Croft asked.

"Going in, yes. Goggles, hoods, latex gloves, the works. When you're wearing night-vision infrared goggles, you can see them a long time before they can see you. It's just like the training. We take it down by the numbers. No mistakes, remember?"

"Got it," Croft replied.

"DeWitt returned to the circle and sat down. "Everything's ready to roll. My weapons are secure and the other equipment is checked out. What's the drill?"

"Just like I told everybody else. We go in, take it down by the numbers, and get out. No messin' around. Do your assigned job and let's do this thing then make tracks. You all know exactly what to do. Any questions?"

"One," DeWitt said.

"Shoot," Auxton replied.

"Okay, we go in and secure the main floor to the house. You and me go to the basement to hit the vault. What if there's someone down there and we've missed a telephone line or a radio transmission line cable? We could be screwed big time."

"Okay," Auxton said. "When we move inside, Croft and Kelly watch the top levels and the front entrance. If there's anyone on the basement level, we handle them just like everybody else. We hit the vault, you and me. We take all the cash Miles has on hand and place our charges. Face it, what are they going to do, call a cop?"

"I'm satisfied," DeWitt said.

"Okay, anything else before we do it?"

No one replied.

"Okay," Auxton said. He stepped back from the circle and slipped on his throat microphone and the earpiece attached to the portable radio clipped to his belt. Then he slid a solid black hood over his head that covered everything except his eyes, nose, and mouth. When the hood was comfortably in place, he slipped infrared night-vision goggles over his eyes and secured the strap. "Radio silence unless it's life or death or I call you," he said. "VOX only on the radio. Move out to your positions and follow my lead. Let's go hit this bad man where it hurts."

The men fanned out toward Miles's house, each going in a different direction to their assigned positions. The night-vision goggles made mobility in the darkness as easy as in daylight . . . and all without a light source visible to the naked eye. They also lent a strategic advantage to Auxton and his men, allowing them to see men and objects through the darkness long before their intended victims could see them.

Auxton took the point straight up the middle. He worked his way through the thick brush toward the house. It took him five minutes to maneuver his way, but he finally reached the spot he sought and crouched down in the undergrowth. He watched for a long moment to pinpoint the exact location of each of Miles's men he had watched earlier doing roving foot patrol around the perimeter. Then he cut a hole in the security fence and looked down at his watch. In two minutes, the telephone lines and communications cables into the house would be neutralized. The guard on the gate would be dead by now. The radio and telephone in the guard shack would be destroyed. Two roving guards on the side of the house opposite to where he now crouched should also be dead.

He waited and held his breath. One minute. The last

guard approached the steps to the house. Auxton counted the seconds down. Right on the mark, he was up from the underbrush and running toward the guard. He covered half the distance separating him and the unsuspecting man. His silenced H&K MP-5 submachine gun spat fire and death. The silent 9mm rounds caught the guard in the back, shoulders, and neck. He fell to the ground in a sea of crimson that gushed into the air against the light of the house.

Croft rounded the corner of the house at the rear. He saw Auxton and nodded his head to proceed.

Kelly was next, running hard from the front. He gave the go-ahead nod as he ran.

Auxton checked his watch again. DeWitt was fifteen seconds overdue. When he looked up, DeWitt materialized from the darkness in a hard sprint.

Auxton motioned for everyone to move forward.

DeWitt, Croft, and Kelly obeyed immediately. They hit the steps on the run, weapons poised. DeWitt made a single, focused kick into the door just below the lock. It crashed open.

Auxton entered first, the muzzle of his MP-5 searching the interior of the house for a target. A man appeared through a doorway on the opposite side of the room, holding a short-barreled shotgun in his hands. Auxton tapped out a staccato burst of death from the 9mm MP-5. The barrage hit the shooter in midchest and zippered him to his neck. Blood splayed into the air and splattered the floor and walls. The shooter fell two steps from where he had first appeared.

Croft and Kelly moved through the house looking for more of Miles's men. Auxton and DeWitt headed toward the doorway that led to the basement. They hit the door, dislodging it from its hinges, then jumped down the steps toward the hallway below.

When they reached the long hallway that led to Bubba

Ray's operations center, a man appeared from a side door. He was barefoot and wearing only a T-shirt and shorts. He carried a small automatic pistol. He appeared startled to see DeWitt and Auxton. The pistol came up at arm's length, pointed toward the hooded insurgents, but his reaction was far too slow. DeWitt triggered a burst from his silent MP-5 subgun. The man's white shirt and shorts immediately turned red. He stumbled forward and hit the walls. His arm fell to his side and then he lifted it again. He stumbled once more and aimed the gun toward Auxton and DeWitt. A shot roared and the concussion rocked the hallway. Auxton unsheathed a long burst of subgun fire and the bullets pelted into the bloody, dying man. His body vibrated for a long moment before he collapsed into the sticky pool of blood at his feet.

Auxton and DeWitt jumped over the dead man and ran down the hallway until they reached the operations-room door. They kicked it down.

Todd jumped from his chair and landed on the floor. He cowered, his arms shielding his head and face. "Please don't hurt me!" he pleaded. "I'll do anything . . . tell you anything. Please, God, don't hurt me!"

Auxton gestured with the subgun's muzzle. "Open the vault. Do it now!"

"I don't know the combination," Todd screamed.

"Three seconds," Auxton said. "One, two . . ."

"Okay! Don't shoot me. I'll open it." Todd scrambled to his feet and moved toward the vault door. He worked the combination and then moved the handle. The door swung open.

"Good boy," Auxton said. He stared at the stacks of bundled cash inside the giant safe.

"How much is there?" DeWitt asked.

"Two, maybe two and a half million. Are you going to hurt me?"

"Do you run all this for Bubba Ray Miles?" Auxton

asked. He moved the muzzle of the subgun around the room pointing it at walls and racks of computers and electronic equipment.

"Yes," Todd answered nervously.

"And you know what he does? The kind of businesses he operates?"

"Yes," Todd said. He looked nervously toward the ceiling when he heard a series of gunshots from the living area upstairs. "What are you going to do to me? Are you going to hurt me?"

"I'm just going to mete out a little criminal justice," Auxton said. "I'm not going to hurt you. I'm going to kill you."

Todd fell to his knees again, pleading. "No! Please! I'll do anything. Please!"

A burst of scorching orange fire from Auxton's subgun ended Todd's plea-bargain negotiations.

DeWitt was already unloading the vault. He stuffed bundles of money into his backpack until it was full. Then he filled Auxton's backpack while Auxton placed explosive charges around the room. When the vault was empty and Auxton was finished, they shouldered the packs. Then they left the basement control center to the raging hellfire that would soon engulf it and reduce it to ashes.

Croft was waiting on the first floor. Kelly covered the outside perimeter. Auxton and DeWitt burst through the doorway into the room where Croft stood.

"It's done," Auxton said. "And your end?"

"Done. Eleven dead up here . . . total. Charges placed and armed," Croft said.

"Two dead downstairs," Auxton said. "That makes thirteen. One more and we're even. Maybe Miles, before he gets his ticket punched, will get the message that payback is nothing short of pure hell."

"Lowlife punks like you and the nigger boy got to learn that you don't mess with Bubba Ray Miles," Miles said. He stood three feet away and puffed a large cigar, blowing the smoke toward Marc's face. On Miles's face was a deathly expression that Marc had not seen there before. His voice was sadistically cold. "You boys can't just come in heah and rip off mah drugs for your own benefit. Now, are you workin' with somebody else or is this some kind of solo deal?"

Marc Lee stared at Miles through bloodshot eyes, but he didn't speak. His right eye was almost swollen shut from the beating one of the longshoremen had given him minutes before. His knees felt weak and rubbery, useless. His side ached and his guts throbbed from the repeated jabs the big longshoreman had given him. His hands and feet were tied to a large wooden column in the center of the warehouse. Another rope around his chest and midsection held him firmly to the pole. When his head tilted left, he could barely see Carl tied in a similar manner to another wooden pole. He could tell Carl was bleeding badly, hurting. Miles and his band of thugs had stripped them of their shirts and left them naked from the waist up. Marc felt blood oozing from a cut somewhere on the right side of his chest. It stung slightly, but the pain was negligible compared to the others that consumed his brutalized body. He managed to move his head until he looked down squarely into Bubba Ray's eyes. His words came with great effort, but come they did. "It ain't over yet, Miles," Marc said. "No way."

"You're right about that, boy," Bubba Ray said. He turned to Joe McNally, who stood near Carl several feet away. "Joe, come over heah."

"Yes, Sir, Mr. Miles," McNally said. He took three or four steps and stopped beside Bubba Ray. "What?"

"Joe, teach this heah boy a lesson about how to behave when he's dealin' with Bubba Ray Miles."

McNally grunted once and gazed into Bubba Ray's

eyes. "You want I should hurt him or just make him uncomfortable?"

Bubba Ray took a long draw on his cigar and smiled. "Hurt the bastard!"

"Okay," McNally growled, and then he grinned broadly. He interlaced his fingers, stretched his arms, and popped his knuckles. Then he made a hard fist that appeared as large as a cantaloupe at the end of his arm. He stretched hard, drew back, and sent a right jab into the left side of Marc's face. The impact was so hard that the roofing rattled above Marc at the top of the pole.

Marc's head jerked hard to the right and blood trickled from his open mouth. He gasped for breath, closed his eyes, and mentally detached himself from his body.

McNally moved in close now. He hit Marc with a punishing right-left combination to the abdomen. Marc's head flopped loosely now as his body absorbed the brutal impact of the punches.

Breath was hard to draw now, almost impossible. Marc choked, coughed, and gasped, but nothing seemed to work. The breath just wouldn't come. McNally was back and another right-left combination took all the breath from his body this time. Marc went limp.

"Well now, that certainly didn't take you too long, Joe," Bubba Ray said. "Ah thought Marc Lee was tougher than that. Ah guess he's just a pussy with a reputation after all. Let's go over heah and talk to the nigger boy for a minute. See if he's any smarter than his friend."

McNally followed Bubba Ray to the pole where Carl was restrained. Carl was bleeding from facial cuts and, like Marc, lacerations to his upper chest. He was conscious, but badly dazed. He had witnessed the torture McNally had administered to Marc, and when he saw Miles moving toward him, he knew he was heading for a dose of the same bitter medicine.

Miles stopped and stared at Carl's bleeding body.

"Boy, yo' pardner weren't so tough. You dark ones like to fight. Joe heah likes to fight, too. Ahm gonna let him have a piece of yo' ass if you don't tell me some things."

Carl fixed his aching jaw until it was hard set. He stared at Miles through hate-filled eyes and said nothing. He envisioned himself free, his hands around Miles's neck, Miles's eyeballs bulging from his head and his face turning blue black in the instant before he sent him into the lasting darkness of death. But Carl knew he wasn't free, not yet, and Miles now held the upper hand. And surely Bubba Ray Miles intended to administer as much misery as he could before his evil lust for revenge was slaked with the salty taste of blood.

"You're stubborn just like yo' pardner. Lookin' at me like that, ah get the feelin' you're tryin' to act uppity. Ah don't care much for uppity niggers," Miles said. "Joe, give this boy a ass whippin'." Miles stepped back and turned away.

McNally stepped forward and slammed his favorite right-left combination into Carl's stomach. Carl flinched, stiffened. McNally grunted and moved back. He drew a long right hook and sent it into Carl's face. Blood and sweat flew as Carl's head jerked to the left. Carl trembled, his body vibrating with pain. He applied every ounce of mental determination he had and stiffened for the next punch. It came. A solid left hook to the side of the head sent Carl wavering in and out of consciousness. He held on by a thread and pure survival instinct.

"Hold it, Joe," Bubba Ray said. "Go get me that there magnetic crank that ah used for a paper weight over in the office. You know, the one that came out of the old wall telephone. Get me a length of wire, too. Somethin' five or six feet long. Don't make no difference what kind it is."

"You gonna beat the boy with that, boss?" McNally asked.

"Nawsir, ahm gonna shock him into talkin' or pissin' in his pants. Whichever comes first," Miles said.

Carl managed to get his eyes open long enough to see McNally leave the warehouse. Bubba Ray kept his distance, but he watched Carl and listened to him struggle for breath. He found deep satisfaction in the fact that he had both of the tough guys whipped to a pulp. Now it was time to get mean.

McNally returned. He carried a roll of wire in one hand and the old telephone crank in the other. The crank, as Miles called it, looked like three large horseshoe magnets strapped side by side. In the middle of them, the center of their magnetic field, was a coil of wire that looked like an electric motor armature. A small crank with a black handle was attached to a geared wheel that turned the armature inside the magnets. Two screw posts for wires were on the side near the handle. "Here go, boss," McNally grunted. Miles took the small crank generator. He unrolled a piece of wire and wrapped it around one screw post. He cut another piece with his pocket knife and attached it to the second screw post. The wire was bare, so there was no insulation to remove. Miles looked up at McNally. "Heah, Joe, take these wires. Ah want you to hook one of 'em to the boy's wrist. Wrap it around a time or two. Take the other'un and stick it down his pants against his belly. Be sure it's good and close against his skin."

McNally obeyed the orders and stepped back beside Bubba Ray. "What now, boss?"

"Stand and watch the show," Miles said. "Watch the boy dance."

Miles turned the crank, slightly at first. Carl felt the trickle of electrical current hit him. He twitched, but he was in too much pain from McNally's beating to pay much attention.

Miles turned the crank harder, faster. Carl's body

jumped hard and shook from the sharp jolt of the electricity.

Bubba Ray Miles laughed. He stopped for a moment and looked up at Carl. "Sorta tickles, don't it, boy?" he said.

Miles hit the crank harder and faster than he had before. Carl took all he could stand. He screamed.

Marc regained consciousness. He moved his head slightly. Just enough to see Miles doing something to Carl. He heard Carl scream. He tried to unscramble his senses. He ached and he knew he was hurt badly. He also knew he couldn't give up. Wouldn't. He had to find a way to get free. A way to repay Bubba Ray Miles for his torture. Then he remembered. His belt. Yes, freedom was inside his belt. Marc looked through his good eye at his waistline and relief washed over him. His belt was still there. His hands were firmly bound to the sides of the wooden pole, so movement would be difficult. But it wouldn't be impossible. If he could shuffle just another inch, he could get his fingers inside his belt in the rear. And then he could pry open the leather security pouch there, the double layer of the liner inside the belt. If he could do that, he might, just might, get one hand on either the military-issue flat can opener or the small surgical steel scalpel blade he always carried for just such an emergency. But if Bubba Ray Miles or one of his goons detected his movements, Marc knew, unquestionably, both he and Carl were dead men.

Marc slid his hands along the pole until he felt his pants. Then he held his breath and wiggled his fingers toward freedom. Maybe.

Chapter Fifteen

Ronnie Richardson arrived an hour early at the Cottage Hill Road warehouse in west Mobile. He had spent the night in Mobile rather than driving into the country to stay at Miles's farm. His early arrival afforded him a margin of safety before Lee and Browne were due, just in case something went astray. He didn't know that Miles had searched for him all night to inform him that Lee and Browne wouldn't be coming to the warehouse to get weapons. There was no need now that the two newly arrived tough guys had breached Miles's trust.

Richardson unlocked the small door beside the overhead doors and entered. He shut off the security system and switched on the interior lights. He turned to close the door when he heard the roar of an eighteen-wheeler outside. He stepped into the doorway and saw a big Kenworth with a large trailer coming into the lot.

An alarm triggered in Richardson's mind. There were no markings on the truck. It wasn't the same one Lee and Browne had driven the night before. Richardson hesitated, unsure of what he should do. He waited until the truck rolled to a stop in front of the door. A man wearing blue coveralls climbed from the rig on the passenger side.

"Good morning," the man said.

"'Morning," Richardson replied. "I haven't seen you here before. What can I do for you?"

The man was on the ground now. The driver had also climbed out. He was in front of the rig at the fender cowling. "I'm Don Campbell and this is my partner, Fred Hilton. We're here to pick up some illegal weapons and explosives. FBI . . . you're under arrest."

Richardson bolted back through the door, Campbell close behind him. He got three steps inside and found himself face-to-face with three men with automatic weapons. He turned immediately and crashed into Campbell as he tried to escape. He got through the door and onto the steps outside. Hilton was on the ground on one knee with a short-barreled shotgun aimed at the doorway. Richardson jumped the railing and ran across the lot. He hurt his ankle in the jump, but he wasn't about to stop. He reached beneath his jacket and came out with a Sig-226 automatic. He spun and fired two fast rounds at Hilton.

Campbell was on the steps now, a large Smith & Wesson automatic in his hands. "Stop!" Campbell yelled.

Richardson fired two more shots as he ran. He got to the corner of the building and turned to take cover, but another agent with a shotgun confronted him. Richardson fired fast, a pair of hardballers to the head. The agent fell back, dead.

Richardson didn't see the second man. He spun back toward the lot and ran hard in the direction of the gate and his car parked outside.

"Stop!" Campbell yelled for the second time.

Richardson ignored the order. He turned to fire again when he felt multiple blunt impacts slam into his chest. He felt himself falling to the ground and he could do nothing to stop it. The security lights in the lot were growing dim. There was no pain, just the feeling that something brutal had hit him and taken his breath away. He realized his weapon was gone, his fingers numb. And then there were no more thoughts, only still silence and darkness.

"They should have checked in by now," Jill said nervously.

Brittin Crain read the worry on her face and in her eyes. He knew she was right; Marc and Carl should have checked in before now. That meant something had possibly gone wrong somewhere. Maybe. He decided to try to play it down and distract Jill. "They had a lot to do last night. Things can change on the spur of the moment. I'm sure they just got tied up or something. They'll be all right," Crain said. He knew the instant the words left his mouth that he was lying and even he didn't believe for one second what he had said.

Benjamin Jasper looked at his watch. "Maybe if we move on the second warehouse, it'll take your minds off of it," he said.

"He's right," Dianne Oakley said. "Worrying won't do anyone any good. Let's get on with the program."

"You're right," Jill said reluctantly. "Let's go do it."

Crain and Jill got into one car while Jasper and Oakley got into their Trans Am. They drove along the dark streets of Mobile toward Miles's warehouses at Bayside Transportation. When they arrived fifteen minutes later, Agent-in-Charge Harvey Harrison was waiting half a block away in a dark sedan with three other agents. Crain stopped his car and got out to talk with him.

"What's the good word?" Crain asked.

"I just received a call on the cellular phone a few minutes ago," Harrison said. "Our other agents neutralized the warehouse on Cottage Street. Ronald Richardson is deceased. He engaged the agents in a brief firefight in his efforts to escape. Our agents returned fire and he was terminated. No other resistance was encountered. Bubba Ray Miles's weapons are now in federal custody."

"Any sign of Marc and Carl?" Crain asked.

"None," Harrison replied.

"What's the score here?"

"We've had it under surveillance since midnight. There are six men working here, best we can determine. Activity level is moderate; nothing to indicate any degree of excitement," Harrison said.

"My kind of deal," Crain replied. "Let's take this place down. What say?"

"One more thing," Harrison said. His face suddenly became hard, vacant of emotion, worthy of the nickname "Stoneface" he had earned so long ago. "The team assigned to Miles's residence also reported in. They said that when they arrived there, the place was engulfed in fire. Trashed. A total loss. They located several bodies, but Miles was not among them."

Crain was shocked. "Marc and Carl didn't say anything about that. Sounds like we've got some help that we aren't aware of."

"That's what worries me," Harrison said. "It worries me a lot. We'll deal with it later. Right now, it's time to shut this place down."

Marc was afraid to move much more or open his eyes further than tiny slits. The fingers on his left hand probed the edge of his belt at his back. He could feel it, sense it, but he couldn't get into the storage space inside. Any movement detected by Miles or his thugs would summarily terminate any chance of escape from the bitter bowels of the good ole boy's hellhole. He kept hoping Bubba Ray would grow weary of inflicting pain and call it off for a while. He didn't. But worse than the torture was the fact that it now appeared, judging by the dull fingers of light slipping through the dirty windows, to be approaching daylight outside. And at six minutes after eight, with the approach of the Russian weather satellite, Miles Shipping and Drydock

Company would be reduced to incinerated rubble. It would disintegrate amid a fiery cataclysm and fall as refuse into the depths of Mobile Bay.

Marc could see Miles out of the corner of his good eye. He seemed to be getting some kind of sadistic high out of running the electric current through Carl's body. Marc knew the little generator wouldn't cause permanent damage or inflict serious injury, but that wouldn't make the shocks hurt Carl any less. For Carl, there was no escape. Not yet.

Marc moved his fingers between his belt and his pants. He tried to pry open the small leather slit that concealed his emergency instruments. He almost made it, but the door opened and two longshoremen came in.

"Hey boss," one of the men yelled. "Tommy Duncan is here. He says he's got some information from them police computers that you'd better come take a look at."

Bubba Ray stopped cranking and turned to face the man. "What the hell does that boy mean comin' over heah? Some of them po-leese find him over heah, around this company, or me, and they'll have his ass on a silver platter."

"I told him that, boss, but he insists he's got to talk to you. Says its damned important," the man said.

"Oh, all right," Bubba Ray grumbled. "Ah was just startin' to have me some fun. Tell him to go in mah office. Ah'll be over there in a minute."

"Right," the guy said. He left, followed by the man who had come in with him.

"Joe," Bubba Ray said. "Come on over there with me. Ain't no tellin' what that Sergeant Duncan has got stuffed up his sleeve. Ah never have trusted that boy since we put him on the payroll. Somethin' a little bit spooky about him. Furst he comes out to mah house and now he's comin' to mah business. He's s'posed to know better than that."

"Okay, boss," McNally said. "I can break him into little tiny pieces if you want me to."

"If he gets too smartmouthed, you got mah permission to do just that. Ah ain't in the mood for none of his antics this mornin'," Miles said. "Boy feeds me some information from time to time about what them po-leese is up to and then he thinks he can just nose right on in and do whatever it is he pleases. Well, he can't do that with Bubba Ray Miles. Hell no. Ah ain't got to put up with it from the likes of him. Let's go."

Bubba Ray left the wires from the generator attached to Carl. He exited the warehouse through the same dock-side door the two longshoremen had entered a minute before.

Marc looked cautiously around to be sure there was no one left in the warehouse except him and Carl. When he was sure they were alone, he immediately twisted and turned as best he could against the rope restraints. Every twitch of his muscles shot brutal pain through his body. Despite the pain, he knew that if he and Carl were to survive, he had to work himself free.

The ropes cut into his wrists as he wrestled with them. He could feel the burning and then the warm flow of blood from the intense abrasion left by the rope. The blood saturated the ropes until it softened them. Marc stretched hard. His fingers found the pocket inside the belt liner. Then he got two fingers inside it. He felt around, using his much-dulled sense of touch to identify the implements inside. He found the spare handcuff key, then the flat can opener, but he couldn't locate the stainless-steel surgical blade inside its sterile foil wrapper. He knew it was there somewhere. He wiggled his fingertips, probing. Then he stopped suddenly and froze, his heart racing.

Voices. They were on the dock just outside the door.

At first, Marc thought they were coming in. Instead, the men moved past the door and toward Miles's office farther down the dock.

Marc worked as hard as his weakened body could. The

ropes weren't hurting as much now. He felt them, in their blood-soaked condition, stretch. Then the tip of his finger found the foil package. He managed to get it between the tips of two fingers and slide it toward the top of the leather pocket. He held it there and worked his other hand as free as he could until he could touch the tips of his fingers on the opposite hand. It worked. He got the foil package between his fingers and located the fanned edges at the end of the pack. He pulled them by stretching his fingers apart. Then he felt the shank of the small surgical blade. He let go on one end of the foil and slipped his fingers over the dull end of the blade. It took tremendous effort, but he finally got a grip on the little metal device. He let go of the other side of the foil now and shifted his hold to the end opposite the open end on the pack. He applied pressure and the blade slipped free.

Marc paused, held firmly to the blade, and tried to regulate his breathing. He let his body go limp; only the ropes around his chest kept him standing. His legs hurt and his arms and hands ached, but he reached inside himself and found new strength. Two or three deep breaths and he was ready. A twist of his fingers positioned the blade toward his wrists. He moved his hands slowly and methodically to avoid connecting with flesh before he could engage the rope. The little blade touched the rope and Marc moved it back and forth, sawing the strands one at a time. Each second seemed like an eternity. Finally, the first rope fell limp.

Marc flexed his wrist and stretched his fingers, but his left hand was still tied. He managed another deep breath. Then he sawed some more. This time, it took only seconds and the blood-saturated rope fell limp. He stretched his hand once more and it broke free.

There was no time to waste. Marc immediately cut the rope that secured his chest. Then he leaned over to his ankles and removed the last restraint holding him to the pole. He had to free Carl, but first things first. Miles had stashed their weapons in a pile near the doorway. Marc hobbled there and found his Uzi and his Smith & Wesson 5906. He grabbed both his weapons and Carl's. He also retrieved their backpacks and musette bags. His legs felt like soft rubber, but he willed them to move with great difficulty. He went back to Carl, who was now semi-conscious. The big Parker-Imai knife was inside his musette bag. He found it quickly and made short work of the restraints holding Carl. Then he removed the wires Miles had attached to Carl's body. Carl was almost fully conscious now, but had great difficulty standing and even more difficulty talking. Marc supported him with one arm and managed the Uzi with the other.

"Major, snap out of it," Marc said. "Come on, get alive. We've got to get out of here. You've got to help me."

Carl mumbled something unintelligible and stumbled. His eyes opened, then shut again. He staggered with each step. Marc looked at him and saw his eyelids fluttering. Finally, they stopped and Carl squinted hard as if he were trying to see where he was.

"Major, it's me, Marc. Come out of it!"

"Marc, what's happening? Where are we?"

"Come on, bro. Snap out of it. We're in deep crap, that's where we are. You've got to help us get out of here," Marc said. Each word, each breath, hurt with savage intensity. Every time he moved, pain shot through him like vicious bolts of lightning. But he had to go on. He managed to work their way toward a darker part of the warehouse on the south side. There was a door there that led out of the building to a vacant lot near the street.

Carl's eyes opened and rolled around two or three times as he tried to focus. He looked at Marc, not sure he recognized him. Then he took deep breaths and felt reality closing in on him. Gradually and quite painfully, he came back to his senses. "How'd we get loose, Colonel?" he asked.

"It's a long story," Marc said. "Can you walk on your own?"

"I think so. How are you?"

"Not good, but I'll make it. Can you see well enough to shoot if you have to?"

"I can give it a try," Carl said. "You got guns?"

"Yeah, I got them. Listen, we've got to keep quiet. Miles is still around here and his henchmen are all over the place. We've got to make it to the Jeep. Then we've got to get to the rig. Can you do it?"

"Yeah," Carl said. "I can do it. What the hell did he do to us?"

"Later," Marc said. "This place is going to blow sky-high real soon. We've got to get the rig and cover it in case Miles leaves. This door on the south side leads outside. If we can get out, we can make it. Once we're in the open, we've got to move fast and furious or they could see us. You got the strength to do that?"

"I'll make it. Wow, I hurt."

"So do I," Marc replied. "If we don't go on, we're certainly going to die. If Miles's people don't kill us, the explosion will." Marc found Carl's subgun and autopistol. He checked the magazines first and then handed them to Carl. "I'll check the door. If it's clear, we're out of here."

"Okay," Carl mumbled weakly.

Marc opened the door just enough to check the area outside. He saw no one. They slipped outside and ran toward freedom as hard as their waning strength would permit them.

"Are you sure?" Bubba Ray asked. "Somebody blew up mah house?"

"I've confirmed it," Sergeant Duncan said. "The place is a total loss. Blew it up and burned it. Now, look, I'm getting real nervous. This has been real, but I've had enough. I want out. Call this one a freebie. I'm walking. Feds and God only knows what else are everywhere asking questions and snooping. They aren't going to quit. One weak link, a longshoreman, anybody who knows of our arrangement or anything about what happened on the docks, and we all go down into boiling oil. Enough is enough."

"Cain't say ah blame you," Bubba Ray said. "Startin' to look like a nice time for a vacation to the Bahamas." He turned and looked at Joe McNally. "Joe, give the man his severance pay."

"Right, boss," McNally said. He lurched forward and grabbed Duncan by the neck. He shook him and squeezed at the same time. Duncan struggled and managed to get his hands on his service weapon. He cleared leather and tried to snap off a shot into Joe's chest, but the big man wrestled the weapon away and fired one shot point-blank into Duncan's head.

"Ah don't like quitters," Bubba Ray said. "Feed him to the fishes and let's go take care of them truckers."

Chapter Sixteen

Somewhere deep down within every man there is an inner strength. A reserve of energy strapped with willpower and determination. The will to survive. Marc Lee knew that and he forced himself to find that reserve and call it to action. It took everything he could muster to drive the Leeco high-tech overroad rig, but he managed. Carl rode shotgun in the passenger seat. He was still dazed, but was gaining new ground with every passing minute. The electrical current together with the savage beating had taken its toll on him. He, like Marc, hurt badly. Everything in his body, things he didn't know he had, punished him with every heartbeat and with every breath.

Marc's right eye was almost completely swollen shut now. Only a small slit remained to permit light and images to enter and reveal a bloodshot pupil behind the swollen mass of tissue that was his eyelid. And that made driving all the more difficult. Blood caked on his face and chin from the lacerations to his forehead and jaw. The cuts had finally stopped bleeding, but the dried blood was still there. He knew he probably had internal injuries from McNally's punches, possibly even internal bleeding, but he had to go on now. He had long since passed the point of no return. Bubba Ray Miles had to be stopped by whatever means necessary.

Marc decided to roll the rig back near Miles's drydock operation and witness the explosion that would come soon with the approach of the Soviet weather satellite. And if Miles left the place, the fury of hell on eighteen-wheels would taunt him until the devil himself reached out to gather him for the great abyss beyond.

Marc looked at Carl, who still struggled with his ravaged physical condition. "Bro, are you able to operate the weapons systems."

"Man, I don't know. I think I can, but I'm not sure. Maybe with the help of the automatic devices, I can manage it."

"Good," Marc said. "My right eye is becoming more useless by the minute. I don't think I can drive and operate the systems at the same time."

"You feeling any better?" Carl asked.

"Not much. It's hard to operate the brake and clutch because my legs hurt so badly. I can't see worth a damn and every breath feels like a knife blade penetrating my chest. McNally hits hard."

"Damn straight," Carl agreed. "He's like a raging bull. About the same size as one, too. He'll get his. I promise it."

"Maybe we'll get lucky and they'll all be in the building when the Russian bird makes a flyby. If that's the case, they're all done."

"Wouldn't bother me at all," Carl said. "I sure don't feel much like a one-on-one hand-to-hand deal. I guarantee that."

"That's what we've got the technology for. We'll let the computer do as much of the work as we can. You think we need to check in with Brittin before we get back to the drydocks?"

"Yeah. If he's been calling, they're probably wondering if we took a vacation in the middle of all this. I'll ring his bell if you want."

"Do it," Marc replied.

Carl managed to lean forward far enough to reach the noise-canceling Icom microphone. He lifted it from its hanger clip and made the call. "Surfsider, this is Pathfinder. Do you read? Over?"

Several seconds passed before Crain's voice emerged from the Icom speaker. "Surfsider here. Where the hell have you guys been?"

"Sort of tied up," Carl said. "It's a long story we'll share with you sometime. Let it pass for now and say we've had a dose of retribution Bubba Ray Miles style."

"Where are you now?"

"Heading back for the docks at Bubba Ray's. We want to see it when it goes bang."

"Roger that. Here's the update. We've taken Bayside Transportation and made seven arrests. Agents hit the arms stash, killed the Richardson guy in a firefight. They have all of the weapons and other goodies on an eighteen-wheeler headed for the field office in Montgomery. Did you get your end of things taken care of last night?"

"Affirmative," Carl said. "Gonna be a whole bunch of fire and flaming pieces flying real soon. I could recommend a couple places to stay away from this morning. You guys hit any snags?"

"Nothing much," Crain said. "We confiscated more than three million hits of Quaaludes and Dilaudid at Bayside. Problem with all this is we can't put our boy at the scene of any of it. He might own or lease the buildings, but we don't have him with his hand in the cookie jar. We need that if we're going to have a case. You got anything building on your end?"

"Yeah, we can build a case if we can make this intercept from Detroit. I think the bubble is about to burst for Bubba Ray. Over."

"Yeah, I almost forgot. We got word a little while ago that somebody trashed Miles's house in the boonies. Was that you?"

"Trashed it? No, it wasn't us. What happened?"

"Blew it all to hell and left about thirteen people dead. I haven't seen it myself, but the reports we've gotten say it was one big mess."

"Well, well," Carl said. "We got some help in this deal?"

"Apparently," Crain replied. "We'll work on that from this end. You need any help?"

"Negative," Carl said. "We've had a rough night, but I think we can handle it. We'll contact you when there's something to report. You got anything else?"

"Negative," Crain said. "Just watch your backside."

"Count on it," Carl said. He replaced the microphone and turned to Marc. "You got a plan, Colonel?"

"Yeah," Marc said. "We'll go to the lion's den and see if he comes out. If he doesn't, we got him. If he does, then we'll deal with him in whatever manner he dictates."

"Ah don't believe this!" Bubba Ray screamed when he entered the warehouse and found the poles empty. The ropes that had held his captives were lying on the floor, severed. Despite intensive searches, Marc and Carl weren't to be found. "Ain't nobody around this place got no brains 'cept me?"

No one answered. Dull faces stared back at him.

Miles was furious. First his house, and now the men he had enjoyed taunting were gone. And that, he knew, spelled trouble of the worst kind because these two men weren't like any other men he had ever encountered. "Awright, we got to get out of this place. A car is too dangerous. They know it. Joe, get them eighteen-wheelers we got ready to roll. Some of you men gonna have to drive. We got some more ludes and Dilaudid in them crates next door. Load it all on four or five eighteen-wheelers. Don't put it all in one truck in case we lose somebody. You got five minutes and ah want this here place clean as a pin. We got to find them two truckers and put 'em out of mah misery."

"Uh, where we goin', boss?" McNally asked.

"Flawda. Ah got me a condo over there. We can stay there until ah get us out of the country. We gonna have to do it now. Them two truckers is mean. They'll be back and you can bet your sorry asses on that. Now, get a move on. All of you."

The men jumped into action. They looked like ants working for the survival of a large hill. They loaded everything into five trucks, a partial shipment in each.

Miles ordered a crate of automatic weapons, stashed in the warehouse amid drygoods shipments, loaded aboard one of the rigs. He also ordered three of the stolen military-issue M-16s to be made ready for service. He loaded those aboard the rig he chose as his escape vehicle and instructed Joe McNally to drive.

"We all ready to go?" Bubba Ray asked.

Heads nodded in affirmation as the longshoremen-turned-truckers stood on the dock in a tight circle.

"Okay, let's us haul some tail," Bubba Ray said. He bit the tip off of a cigar and spat it on the dock. He lit the cigar and took a deep draw that filled his lungs with pungent smoke. "Awright, take Interstate ten and keep the two-way on. Ah'll give you directions after we get out of Alabam. You see anythin' that looks suspicious, yell on your radio. Keep your eyes peeled for them two truckers. If they show, kill 'em deader than hell."

Marc parked the rig two blocks from Miles Shipping and Drydock. He could see the area clearly along the front street that provided the only possible exits. If anyone left the buildings, they would have to go either north or south. A tattered building shielded the rig from view. Only the long nose of the custom conventional tractor protruded beyond the corner of the building. The high-definition television was rolling, monitoring every movement made along the street. With the zoom capabilities of the cameras, a close-up view of the front of Miles's buildings was possible.

Marc looked at his wristwatch. Two minutes after eight o'clock. That meant hell was coming to Miles Shipping and Drydock Company in five more minutes. The infrared scanning imager showed a flurry of activity along the docks and inside the building. The heat images of people moving around reflected on the computer screen. So far, no one had shown on the street.

"Strange," Marc said. "No one has tried to leave."

"Maybe we overlooked something," Carl said.

"What's that?" Marc asked.

"He could load everything on a boat and leave across the bay."

"I don't think so," Marc said. "Miles doesn't have a boat here. Besides, the water would make him too vulnerable to the Coast Guard. To get out into the ocean, he'd have to clear the Coast Guard base on McDuffie Island. He wouldn't want that. I figure he's running scared right about now. He'll leave by road if he leaves at all. Maybe we'll get lucky and he'll sit tight for three more minutes. That's all we need now. It's three minutes after eight."

The blunt nose of an International cab-over tractor slid into view at the edge of Miles's building. Marc caught it on the video monitor first. He looked hard with his good eye and then turned back to the camera image. "We got movement," he yelled.

Carl jerked his attention to the building. "Just the one?"

Marc looked back at the infrared imager. "No, I see five, maybe six, judging by the heat trails showing on the screen. He's moving out."

"What now?" Carl asked.

"Hit first. Hit last," Marc replied. "Let's roll."

"Okay, roll 'em," Carl said.

Marc fired the powerful diesel engine and dropped the rig into gear. He moved out onto the street and headed toward Miles's building. The International was in the street now. Behind it, a Kenworth rolled onto the blacktop.

"Bring up the rockets and take out the trailer on the International," Marc yelled.

Carl worked switches until the weapons screen appeared on the CRT. He donned the optical sight helmet and watched the International snake along the road. Then he adjusted the laser sight until it fell on the rear undercarriage of the International's trailer. "Here we go," he yelled. His finger touched the firing mechanism and the Leeco rig rumbled. A loud whoosh preceded a trail of white smoke and fire as the Hellfire-class missile streaked toward destruction.

The International's trailer jumped skyward from the ground in the microinstant after the Hellfire bird slammed into it. A raging fireball evolved and sent fire and smoke skyward in a cyclonic ball. Debris rained down on the Kenworth and the roof of Miles's building.

The driver of the Kenworth was momentarily stunned. He braked hard, stopped. Then he caught another gear and floored the accelerator. The Kenworth came back to life and crunched its way through the fiery debris.

"Let's take him and get out of Dodge," Marc shouted. "That place is going to blow at any second."

"Roll!" Carl yelled.

Marc floored the accelerator and the mighty Leeco machine roared to life. He changed gears quickly and built speed. When he reached the burning International, he cut right and avoided as much of the trash as he could. The Kenworth was ahead now, rolling full-steam.

"Three more coming out behind us," Carl yelled when the Leeco rig sped past the alley leading to Miles's docks. "Looked like McNally in the lead machine. The Peterbilt."

"Probably got Bubba Ray with him," Marc said. He

chanced a glance into the rearview mirrors. "They're coming after us."

"His mistake," Carl said.

The Kenworth headed toward Interstate 10. The driver was frantic. He drove the rig along the tattered street like an amateur. He careened from one side of the street to the other and back again.

Marc changed gears and closed the gap. Every move he made to steer the rig caused renewed pain to consume his body. When he floored the clutch, moving his legs, the pain intensified. He stayed with the Kenworth despite it all.

"Got him in the sight," Carl said.

"Hold it on," Marc replied. "When he makes the intersection up ahead, trash him."

The Kenworth roared into a three-way intersection and Carl pressed the firing mechanism. A three-second burst of 20mm cannon fire pelted into the back of the rig. The projectiles tore through aluminum and ate the rubber on the rear tires. The Kenworth careened right, out of control, crashed through a barricade, and sailed cab-first into the choppy waters of Mobile Bay."

"Nice shooting," Marc said. He glanced once more into the rearview mirrors. "Three of them behind us. Let's see what they're made of." He turned the rig left onto a connecting street, drove several blocks, and then turned right onto the entry ramp to Interstate 10 eastbound.

"You going across the bay?" Carl asked.

"You got it," Marc replied. He cut into traffic and moved into the through lane. He realized he was having difficulty with depth perception due to the injury to his right eye. He looked hard into the mirrors, a double take, and then he floored the accelerator. "If we can get far enough ahead of them, we can wait on the other side of the bridges and take them before they cross. When we get through the tunnel, we'll make a decision."

"It's still rush hour," Carl said. "It's a blessing that most of the traffic is coming into town rather than going out. I don't want to see innocent people hurt. There's been enough of that by Miles's drugs."

"Here comes the tunnel," Marc said. "Hang on, I'm going to roll these eighteen-wheels hot and hard."

"Drive this damned thing, Joe," Bubba Ray screamed. He lifted the CB radio microphone and yelled into it. "Awright, boys, they're in the tunnel. Catch 'em and shoot the hell out of 'em. Don't let 'em get across this bridge."

Bubba Ray and Joe were in the rocking chair in their conventional Peterbilt. There was one truck ahead and one behind them. Joe changed gears and descended into the tunnel beneath a portion of Mobile Bay. He kept his eyes on the taillights of the Volvo-White rig in front of them. Behind them, the headlights from a Mack tractor glared into the rearview mirrors.

Bubba Ray yelled into the microphone again. "Albert, bring that big old Mack on around us while we're in this heah tunnel. Me and Joe will bring up the back door. Ya'll go on up there and one of you get in front and the other one behind that there rig them boys is in. We can shut 'em down thataway. Come on."

"I got a grip on that, Bubba," Albert answered. "Get that old Petercar outta mah way. I'm a-comin' through."

Joe pulled the Peterbilt as far to the right as he could get without hitting the sides of the underwater tunnel. He looked in his left mirror and saw the headlights from the Mack closing on him. Another glance, and they were beside him.

"Heah we go, Bubba," Albert yelled.

The Mack and its forty-two foot trailer cleared the front of Bubba Ray's Peterbilt. It closed hard now on the taillights of the Volvo-White just ahead.

Bubba lifted the mike again. "This heah is Bubba Ray.

Billy, are you and John Paul over there on the east side of the bridge?"

"Ro-gur, ro-gur, Mr. Bubba Ray," Billy said over the CB. "Me and John Paul be waitin' on the east side, all right. What do you want us to do?"

"Ah want you to get that traffic cleared out. Get over in the eastbound lane and start movin' onto the west. Thin them four-wheelers out. We got them ole boys in a vise now. 'Less they can swim mighty fine, they ain't no way for 'em to go."

"What about all the cars, Bubba?" Billy asked.

"They'll get outta yo' way when they see them eighteen wheels rollin at 'em. Keep one of them lanes clear until you see that big ole shiny red conventional rig with LFL on it. When you got 'em in sight, shut both lanes down so's they got nowhere to go. We'll come up from the back door and handle things from there. Come on."

"Ro-gur, Mr. Bubba Ray," Billy shouted. "Me and John Paul be a-rollin' hammer down westbound in the eastbound lanes. Gonna shut them tough guys down."

Marc looked into the rearview mirrors and saw the beige Volvo-White closing hard, passing a line of traffic. Behind it now, the Mack from Bubba's shipyard came on strong. It moved in behind the Volvo-White. The Peterbilt, the one Carl had seen driven by Joe McNally, closed on the Mack and brought up the rear. The rigs were out of the tunnel now and onto the bridge that spanned the Mobile Bay. Beneath them the water of the bay was choppy from gusting winds. Waves rolled across the surface like predetermined cyclic oscillations. The bridges shook with the force of the explosion at Miles Shipping and Drydock a mile and half away. And that, Marc knew, meant Bubba Ray's waterfront death shop was closed forever.

"Guess that was that," Carl said. "Sorry we missed it."

"Me, too, but there's no time to enjoy it. Here they come," Marc shouted. "You on line with the goodies?"

"Got it. Got the Volvo-White in the sights," Carl replied.

"Wait until they're on our back door real solid, then give them something to think about," Marc said.

"Affirmative," Carl replied. He watched the Volvo-White closing the distance between the rigs. Carl kept his eyes locked on the target screen in the optic sight. He chanced a quick glance occasionally into the video monitor to see what the HDTV showed. The Volvo-White was closer now, thirty or forty feet off the rear bumper of the Leeco rig. "Coming on strong," Carl yelled.

"Whenever you're ready," Marc said. His vision was blurring now in his good eye. He took his left hand off the steering wheel and rubbed his eye just long enough to make it clear.

Carl zoomed in with the HDTV camera mounted in the rear of the trailer. "He's talking on the CB. Let's see if I can find him." He leaned over and twisted the channel selector on the Cobra CB until he heard the strong signal of the Volvo-White coming through the speaker.

"I'm goin' around them assholes, Bubba Ray," the driver said.

"Take 'em out!" Bubba Ray shouted. "Box 'em in, whatever you can do. Billy and John Paul be comin' from the other side."

"Great," Carl said. "Did you hear that?"

"Yeah," Marc replied. "I don't see them coming yet. You watch the back on the HDTV. I'll cover the front."

"The White's on us," Carl shouted just as gunfire sent projectiles pelting into the rear of the Leeco machine.

"Take him!" Marc yelled.

Carl checked the optic sight and pressed the firing trigger. A pair of scorching rockets left the rear pods and slammed into the nose of the Volvo-White. The bridge shook from the massive concussion. A massive ball of cleansing fire appeared behind the rig in the video monitor. The Volvo-White catapulted left and careened over the lip of the bridge into the waters of Mobile Bay.

Traffic had disappeared in the eastbound lanes. Marc looked ahead as far as he could see with his defective vision. "Here they come. Two of them in eighteen-wheelers."

Carl jerked around and aligned the optic sight. He triggered a pair of deadly birds from the front cowl pod. Streaks of white smoke marked a trail of death toward the rigs driven by Billy and John Paul. The birds hit at almost the same time. Raging torrents of fire rose from the roadway ahead and sent charred rubble airborne toward the marshy ground beneath the bridge.

The Mack had cleared the wreckage behind them now. Carl checked the HDTV and locked onto the charging big rig. He set the optic sight to the rearview and aligned on the nose of the big Mack truck.

"Bye, bye, bulldog," he said. He let go another Hellfire-class missile. The stream of white smoke and fire marked the death trail that ended in the disintegration of the Mack and its occupants. The rig went skyward in a cataclysmic funnel of scorching death.

"One to go," Carl said.

Marc slowed the rig and let it drift to a stop.

Carl lifted the CB microphone and spoke. His face was tight with vengeance and his voice more icy cold than the winter waters of Mobile Bay. "Bubba Ray, it's just you and us now. How good are you?"

There was no answer, but the big Peterbilt drifted to a stop a hundred feet behind the Leeco rig.

Marc climbed out, his Uzi in his right hand. He stood beside the rig and stared hard at Bubba Ray and Joe McNally behind him.

Carl climbed out also. He extended the cable that attached the optic-sight helmet to the control console. He held the trigger mechanism for the weapons systems in his hands.

For a long moment, McNally and Bubba Ray sat still. Then Bubba Ray broke the silence. "Go kill them bastards, Joe."

McNally looked at Bubba Ray and words choked from his mouth. "Right, boss." He climbed from the rig, an M-16 in his hands. He stopped beside the rig and brought the weapon up to fire.

A swarm of killer hornets emerged from the Leeco nest and sent .223 Stinger sizzlers in a deadly barrage that reduced McNally to perforated dead meat before he knew what hit him.

Bubba Ray panicked. He climbed toward the driver's seat and kicked the rig into gear. He moved forward toward the Highway Warriors and his destiny.

Carl gritted his teeth. "Retribution Lee and Browne style, asshole," he said. He fingered the firing mechanism and triggered four simultaneous Stinger missiles from the concealed rear pods. The missiles found their mark at the front of Bubba Ray's Peterbilt. In the heartbeat it took for the missiles to ignite, Bubba Ray Miles and his criminal empire were consumed by the cleansing fires of unforgiving justice. The residue from the explosion rolled skyward and into the dark water of Mobile Bay.

"I don't know who you *really* are or who you work for," Dianne Oakley said. "You do damned good work. Miles is shut down, gone forever. Thank you for that. When we met you two weeks ago, I never would have believed it. I'm impressed."

"Yeah," Benjamin Jasper said. "The system failed. We had a dirty cop and that's taken care of also. He got what he deserved. He was found floating in Mobile Bay."

"Many outstanding people in Mobile," Brittin Crain said. "Zave Auxton got that two-and-a-half-million-dollar

donation for the families of the men slain on Miles's docks.
I think it was great. Mighty decent of somebody."

"We owe a great deal to Marc and Carl here," Jill said.
"Without them, this Alabama bloodbath could have been
much worse than it was. You people have a number of
people in custody. We've cleaned out some dirty truckers
and a number of criminal dock workers. Thomas Barton will
spend the rest of his life in prison for his part in it all. He's
screaming duress, but no judge would ever believe his
story."

"The money Auxton had 'donated,'" Carl said, "won't
bring the loved ones back, but it will sure help ease the
financial burden for them. Question is, who hit Miles's
house."

No one answered.

"Let's leave it at this," Marc said. His black eye shone,
but he smiled. "If my gut is right, and I think it is, maybe
sometimes in order to achieve real criminal justice you
have to be just a little bit criminal. Something tells me Zave
Auxton would know about that, but I'm not going to be the
one to ask him."

ACTION ON EIGHTEEN WHEELS!

Here's a special preview of Book #12
in the OVERLOAD series

VEGAS
GAMBLE
by
Bob Ham

The Vegas mob has put a hit on the owner of a
local trucking company in order to muscle in on
his business. But the dead man was a friend of
Marc Lee's father, and the men of OVERLOAD
mean business, too. Their war on crime has just
become a private vendetta!

Look for OVERLOAD
wherever Bantam Books are sold.

Marcus Lee had not visibly moved a muscle for months. The last time he had, it was only a twitch and perhaps involuntary. He had been comatose since the night so long ago when Bruno Segalini cut off his ear with a short saber and brutalized him. That was in Lee's office at Leeco Freight Lines in Dallas, Texas, and it was the single event that started a war that now knew no end against heartless, savage criminals. That war had consumed, then dominated, the life of Marc Lee, Marcus's son, and of his friend Carl Browne. Both men were ranking Delta Force soldiers home on leave when the savage onslaught destroyed both Leeco Freight Lines and the Lee family home. Marc's mother, Marcus's wife, Helen, had died in the violent retribution initiated by the New York organization ruled by the iron hands of the Segalini family. Marcus had survived in intensive-care safe houses used by the United States government to house federally protected witnesses during criminal trials. Since the night of his injury, he had not been without the custodial care of twenty-four-hour-a-day nurses. Although he was lost in a dark abyss of comatose sleep, Marcus Lee was never alone.

Marcus was a huge man. Even into his early sixties, he had retained his strong physique. When the brutal sleep overtook him, his mind had been sharp and honed with years of experience in the business of moving freight from one part of the United States to another. He had built his Dallas empire with a strong will, strong back, and adventurous mind. He had taken Leeco Freight Lines from a dream to a vastly successful reality through hard work, determination, and a large degree of stubbornness. And until the night the thugs from the mob came to make their final call, he had recouped handsome financial remuneration from his efforts.

A team of doctors provided secretly by the president of the United States as part of a deal with Marc Lee and Carl Browne, had maintained constant watch over the elder Lee's condition. The prognosis was simple: the man could live another twenty years and never come out of the coma or he could wake up tomorrow. Problem was, that tomorrow had never come. And now, many close to the Lee family feared it never would.

Marc and Carl, Jill Lanier, and family friend Brittin Crain all feared Marcus was doomed to an eternal sleep that would someday cause him to cross some slim invisible line that separated him from the permanent darkness of death. And if he did, would he be better off for it? For if Marcus Lee were to awaken, what would he think of the changed world that awaited him? Could he cope with the loss of his wife? His brother? Would he know the Dallas that now saddled the flatlands of northeastern Texas? And what would he think of the arrangement his son had made with the president himself? Would he even know who the president was? Would he approve of the arrangement, or think it not becoming of a member of the Lee family? Most of all, would Marcus Lee even want to live in the changed world that revolved just beyond the outer surface of his coma? If he could make the choice himself, would Marcus choose the certainty of death over the uncertainty of the life that awaited him with the opening of his eyes?

The questions were many, but the answers were few. Even the nurses who had once been so full of hope for his awakening now seemed lost in a complacency as deep as the coma itself. They ran the fundamental vital-signs check every hour. They adjusted the IV drips that fed nourishment into the sleeping giant's body. And when one liquid bag was empty, they hung another beside the bed to ensure that life-sustaining fluids reached his system with ritual regularity. The nurses bathed Marcus Lee and changed his bed linen. They even exercised him without his help or knowledge by moving his legs, massaging his arms and hands and working his feet and toes to stimulate voluntary movement. But even with the best care in the world, the elder Marcus Lee became older and his muscles degenerated from lack of consistent use. The sleeping giant lost his massive vitality a little more every day and he didn't even know it.

Janet Donald knew it. She had watched, nurtured, and cared for Marcus Lee five days a week for the last year and a half. The job provided her with a quiet environment to study. She spent her off time working on her master's degree in nursing. She welcomed the silence. Sometimes, like tonight, she caught herself talking to him while she changed IV drips or bathed him.

"Marcus, are you ever going to wake up?" she asked while she adjusted the flow of the Ringer's IV. The grip had been slowing somewhat earlier in the evening, but now it appeared to have increased. "I guess not. You wake up and I'm out of a job." She laughed. "That's selfish, isn't it?"

Janet looked at the cardiac monitor. The pace had increased also. And that, she knew, wasn't normal. It wasn't serious enough to be concerned about, but there was a change. If it continued, one of the doctors who made the regular morning visits could take a look at the EKG tape and make recommendations.

"Marcus, are you dreaming hard or something?" she asked. She moved his arms and massaged them. They felt alive, but deathly still. "Your heart's been looking good through all this. Don't you go and pull a cardiac arrest on me. You'd disappoint a lot of people. You've got some very nice people pulling for you. Don't die and let them down."

Sometimes she felt silly talking to a comatose man. She had never known Marcus Lee before his injury. That didn't matter. She knew him now probably better than he had known himself or ever would, for that matter. She knew every line of his body, every crease of his skin. She knew his heart rate, respiration, and temperature. More important, she knew, believed, he heard her talking to him. There was something inside her that told her he did. Just because he didn't answer, couldn't answer, didn't mean his brain did not perceive what was going on around him. Sure, maybe he couldn't rationally interpret it, but she knew deep within her soul that Marcus Lee heard and understood. At least sometimes.

Janet finished the IV check and scanned the large bank of electronic equipment attached to Marcus's body. Everything looked all right, so she turned to leave the room. And then Marcus's left leg stiffened beneath the white sheet. It relaxed, quivered for a long moment, and stiffened again. Then his right arm moved from his side and slammed across his chest.

Janet checked the monitors. His heart rate had jumped ten beats per minute, as if he were excited. His respiration increased beyond any point she had seen since she had been with him, and was irregular. That meant, without question, something was happening. She grabbed the hot-line telephone that would ring her straight through to Dallas General. When the voice answered, she spoke calmly. "Get Dr. Collier over here immediately. Something is going on with Mr. Lee. He's moving and his heart rate has increased dramatically. Send a Code Blue trauma team also. He could be on the verge of cardiac arrest. I don't know. I do know something is happening here. Make it stat!"

* * *

Marc Lee was sure the hijackers would come. They had hit the parking lot of the truckstop twelve times in the past sixty-one days. If they were still looking for a free ride to steal, the best diagnosis of their modus operandi indicated it was time for them to make another appearance.

Marc sat comfortably in the cab of the highly customized Leeco overroad rig. The giant Caterpillar diesel power plant beneath the hood of the gleaming red conventional tractor idled a perfectly synchronized tune. Marc watched the color CRT monitor attached to the High Definition Television cameras panning the parking lot. The cameras were integral units concealed in strategic locations around the custom trailer attached to the fifth wheel of the tractor. From the outside, the cameras were almost impossible to spot when they were functioning, when they were off-line and the mechanical port holes closed, they were completely invisible to the untrained eyed.

Carl Browne, Marc's partner in his war against the criminal menace that plagues America, sat across the truckstop parking lot in a red Jeep Cherokee. He watched each movement around the truckstop on a thermal infrared imager concealed in the Jeep's grille.

Marc and Carl, both former Delta Force commandos now Highway Warriors on a campaign against crime in America, had been in the parking lot since just before dark. And now it was almost two o'clock in the morning. But they were used to long tedious hours of waiting and watching. Criminals seldom kept convenient schedules and the truckstop hijackers showed no promise of breaking the trend.

Carl made the radio call first. "This may prove to be a wasted night, Colonel," he said into the microphone of his Icom U-400 UHF transceiver.

Marc picked up the microphone in the cab of the Leeco rig and pressed the talk switch. "It's not over yet, Major. Still a long time before the sun shines. They could still come."

"Affirmative," Carl said. "I hope they do."

"Affirmative. There doesn't seem to be as much activity around this place as there usually is. That could be a deterrent for them. Might spook them."

"Roger," Carl said. "Wait a minute. We got something coming in over at the truck entrance. A faded red Dodge van. We may have some action. Stand by while I scope 'em out."

"Roger, I can't see anything from here. Keep me updated," Marc replied.

"Okay," Carl said. "They're moving toward the parked rigs. Here we go. We got two guys in the front seats and some movement in the back. I can't tell how many are in there. Hang tight."

"Say the word," Marc replied. "I still don't see them. You think it's our boys?"

"Could be. They're moving slowly along the row of parked eighteen-wheelers. They're up to something," Carl replied.

"Description sure fits," Marc said. "If it isn't our boys, they could be looking to make a dope deal. I'm ready on this side whichever way it goes down."

Carl slipped down low in the seat of the Cherokee when the Dodge van turned at the end of the row of eighteen-wheelers and headed back toward him. The headlights from the van fell directly in his eyes. He changed his attention to the infrared imager screen to avoid becoming totally blinded by the glaring lights. He watched as the van moved slowly back along the parked overroad machines, scanning them as if they were looking for something in particular.

Then it stopped. One man left the front of the van

and another climbed from the sliding side door. They ran quickly toward an idling black conventional Kenworth with a reefer trailer attached to its fifth wheel. The words painted in giant letters along the side of the trailer read TYSON'S CHICKENS.

One of the men climbed the step and held the rail while he worked something into the lock below the cab-door handle. The other man disappeared to the rear of the trailer and cut the heavy padlock on the door latch with a pair of bolt cutters. He tossed the lock to the pavement and motioned to the man on the side of the cab.

Carl held his breath and waited until the time was right. He lifted the Icom microphone carefully and spoke slowly. "Okay, Colonel, we've got a hit. Looks like they're our boys. They're taking the Tyson Chicken Kenworth. It's two rows in front of you and three from the highway. We've got one man in the cab. One did a number on the lock at the back, best I could tell. I couldn't see him, but that's my guess. At least one in the van. The driver. As soon as they mount up and make a move for the highway, it's party time. You on over there?"

"Systems armed and ready to go. When they make a move, I'm rolling. You've got the visual, so you call the numbers," Marc replied.

"Okay, steady. The guy from the back of the rig is moving back to the van. That's two in the van and one inside the Kenworth. You want to play it like we planned or do you want to just take them down and be done with it?" Carl asked.

"By the numbers," Marc replied. "These guys have to be moving these shipments somewhere close by. I don't think they'd chance running them too far on the highway. It's much too risky. You tail the van, I'll hang with the Kenworth. Something gets out of whack, take the turkey down. I'll do likewise. Give 'em all the rope you can before you tighten the noose. Over."

Roger," Carl replied.

"I'm moving now," Marc said. "I'm going to get into position at the end of the first row back from them. I don't want to give that guy too much lead. I'll hang back on the fringes until he's moving out of the slot and then I'm on him. Is that a roger?"

"Roger," Carl replied. "I didn't detect any weapons, but you can bet your backside they're carrying somewhere. These guys don't look too much like the upper rungs of the social ladder to me." Carl peeked over the lip of the Jeep's dashboard and the headlights still glared toward him. He managed to cover the glare and take a look with his naked eye. He could see silhouettes, but he couldn't make out anything distinctive about any of the men from the red Dodge van.

"Affirmative," Marc replied. He laid the microphone across his leg and slid the Leeco machine into gear. He let the clutch out slowly and moved from the parking slot he had occupied since just after dark. He let the machine move into the lane between other parked eighteen-wheelers and then he turned it left. When he reached the end of the row of parked overroad machines, he cut hard right and made his way along the drive toward the edge of the pavement. He stopped facing the highway and made one final weapons check of the Leeco rig's on-board high-technology weapons systems. All systems checked functional and armed. He lifted the mike back toward his mouth and called Carl. "I'm in position and ready."

"The van's rolling!" Carl yelled. "Rig's moving, too. I'm on the van. The rig is all yours. Here we go. Showtime!"

* * *

The faded red Dodge van turned right onto the highway and sped ahead. Carl gave it five seconds and followed in the Jeep Cherokee. When he entered the highway, he glanced into the rearview mirror and saw the black Kenworth eighteen-wheeler rolling behind him. Farther back, Marc moved forward in the Leeco custom overroad rig and paced the Kenworth.

Carl made visual contact with the van dead ahead, then pressed the accelerator. The high-performance Chevrolet Corvette 350-cubic-inch 370-horsepower engine jerked the machine to life. He easily closed the gap between him and the van, but he was cautious to stay back far enough so that the driver of the van wouldn't know he was being followed. He lifted the noise-canceling Icom microphone from the cradle and called Marc. "We're on the main highway. The boy skipped the turn onto the interstate. He's going local with this one. Over."

"Roger, let him go," Marc said. "The Kenworth is right behind you now. I'd say we're a half mile back. He isn't getting in any hurry just yet. Stay on the van. They're surely headed for the same place. Probably got a warehouse or storage facility somewhere nearby. If anything happens back here, I'll let you know. Over."

"Affirmative," Carl replied. "Okay, he's turning onto the highway parallel to the interstate. Route Eight. They're going to keep off the beaten path. We're southbound now. I'm going to back off so he doesn't make me. Over."

"Roger," Marc said. "The Kenworth is coming on strong. He's southbound on eight now also. Give them a couple miles and let's do a flip-flop. I'll move ahead of the Kenworth and take the van. You pull off and drop back on the Kenworth. We don't want these solid citizens to get suspicious just yet."

"Roger," Carl replied. "You say the word."

Marc watched the Kenworth move steadily south on Route Eight. He stayed back a quarter of a mile and held the pace. He could tell the driver was oblivious of his presence. Route Eight was used frequently by truckers who wanted to avoid the scales on the interstate in the middle of the night. It wove and twisted for miles, but it eventually made its way back to the interstate highway thirty miles south of the truckstop. Another eighteen-wheeler dodging the scales wouldn't appear unusual to the hijackers who obviously knew the area.

Several minutes passed and Carl lifted the microphone again. "I see an all-night service station up ahead. You want to do the flip there?"

"Roger," Marc replied. "I'm going to overtake the Kenworth now. As soon as he passes the service station, he's all yours. Over."

"Affirmative. I'm in the lot now, pulling up to the gas pumps. Take the van."

Marc pressed the pedal hard and the big Leeco machine shot passed the Kenworth. Marc threw his hand up at the driver in a goodwill gesture as he passed. The driver returned the wave nonchalantly and kept a steady speed. In seconds, Marc was in front of the stolen eighteen-wheeler. He saw the taillights of the van a half mile ahead. He closed hard and then settled in at the same speed the van was rolling. He spoke into the Icom microphone. "I got the van. You on the Kenworth yet?"

"Pulling from the lot now. Kenworth's moving toward you. I think we did a number on them. Over."

"Roger," Marc replied. Brake lights flashed on the van and the driver signaled for a right turn. Marc swerved into the left lane and passed the Dodge. He glanced hard to his right and saw a dead-end sign on the street. He immediately lifted the mike again. "Van's turning off on a road to the right. I think it's a dead end," he said.

"Roger that," Carl replied. "Kenworth's slowing also. He's signaling. This could be more of a dead end than they know."

"I'm going past and turn around," Marc said. "Cut your lights and move in there once the eighteen-wheeler is off the highway. Give them a quick scan with the infrared and let's see what's going on over that hill. Over."

"Roger," Carl replied. "There's a sign on the road that says Southside Consumer Warehouse. I think we've found the place."

Marc drove for another mile before he found a place to turn the rig around. He made the change and headed north on Route Eight. When he reached the road, he slowed the rig and cut his headlights. He called Carl to verify his position. "You on the road to the warehouse, Major?"

"Affirmative. I got them on the scanner. I'm a quarter of a mile off the main highway at the top of the hill. We got two vans now. They met someone else down there. The rig is backing into a loading dock. Over."

"I'm on my way. Don't start without me."

"No, wait," Carl said excitedly. "Change of plans. We got us another eighteen-wheeler down there also. Could be another shipment or a mule for the stuff they just stole. He came from the darkness at the end of the warehouse complex. We're going to have to play this one cool. They've got all kinds of surprises."

Marc eased the Leeco overroad up beside Carl in the Jeep Cherokee. He set the parking brake, kicked the gearshift into neutral, and climbed from the cab. He went to the driver's side of the Cherokee.

Carl rolled the window down and glanced out at Marc. "What's the plan?" he asked.

"Give them five minutes to get involved in their work and we'll pay them a little unsociable social call. I'll go in first just like I'm bringing in another load for one of the warehouses. When I'm in place, you come in. I'll make the first move. You mop up any stragglers or good ole boys with rabbit in their blood."

"Sounds good to me," Carl said.

"Okay, watch your backside. I'm rolling."

Marc climbed back aboard the rig. A minute later, he cleared the top of the hill and descended into the warehouse complex. The instant his headlights fell on the people at the loading dock, he could see a flurry of activity. He lifted the microphone and pressed the talk switch. "They're hustling. They see me and they sure don't like company. Better move on into position."

"Behind you," Carl replied.

Marc positioned the Leeco rig with the long nose of the conventional tractor pointed directly at the loading dock. He switched on his high-beam headlights and climbed from the cab. He carried his silenced Uzi beside his right leg as he walked toward the dock. He was thirty feet from it when a rough voice shouted at him.

"Hey, you. Whatta you want?"

Marc scrutinized the area and then he answered, "I'm sort of lost. I'm looking for the warehouse for Showalter's Material Handling Corporation. You guys know where that is?"

"Ain't never heard of it. This here's a private warehouse. You'd best go look someplace else," the guy yelled.

"Yeah, I'll do that," Marc said. He turned to his right to keep the Uzi hidden. He moved slowly back to his tractor and climbed aboard. He saw the men loading frozen chickens from the rig to the dock. Another team shifted the same thing from the stolen Kenworth to the second eighteen-wheeler. He lifted the Icom microphone and called Carl. "I count seven men. They're working fast and furious. They aren't a very sociable bunch. I'm moving on them now."

"Roger," Carl said. "I'm on your back door."

Marc lifted the microphone to the public-address system and pressed the switch. "You inside the warehouse. The hijackers. You have fifteen seconds to come out with your hands in the air or we'll come in after you."

Gunfire answered his demands.

"I guess that means no," Marc mumbled. "That's a bad decision." He returned the first volley from the Stinger miniguns mounted in the cowling of the Leeco machine. The first swarm of sizzling hornets stung into the tires of the second eighteen-wheeler. The tires ruptured and instantly deflated. Then a dozen death pellets hit the windshield of the Leeco machine. The ballistic glass reduced the intended death rounds to lead and copper fragments that dissipated into the air.

Carl slid to a stop in the Cherokee just past the Leeco machine. Long tongues of fire spat from the muzzles of the miniguns mounted on the Jeep. His hostile projectiles raked the surface of the dock and sent the shooters fleeing for cover. "Give 'em some hellfire," Carl yelled.

"Hellfire going right up the main chute. Stand by," Marc replied. He moved the weapon control and retracted the port rocket pod. Then he steadied the optic sight on the open dock door and triggered a missile. The whoosh hardly had time to become recognizable before the front of the warehouse was consumed in raging fire. Debris flew skyward and lit the night, silhouetting the shooters against a backdrop of flaming ruins.

Marc lifted the PA microphone once more and spoke into it. "Okay, guys, time's up. Now we're going to get serious."

Three men stumbled from the fiery warehouse with

their hands over their heads. They made their way across the lot while Carl covered them with an M-16.

Carl directed them with the muzzle of the autogun and shouted. "Face down on the pavement, all you Long John Silvers. Your pirating and hijacking days are done."

Marc covered the building, but nothing else moved inside. He climbed from the rig and joined Carl. "How many still alive inside?" he asked.

"We're it," one of the men mumbled. "You killed everybody else. Who the hell are you guys?"

Marc smiled. "For common thieves like you, we're death on eighteen wheels."

A savage novel of high adventure

RUN WITH THE DEVIL
by Dan Schmidt

Years ago Sgt. Ben Williams told the sick truth about the massacre at Du Choc -- a grim tale of guilt and genocide that shocked the nation. A dozen war criminals went to jail. But now they're out...combat-tough former marines, who have waited a long time for a piece of Ben's hide.

Backed by the megafirepower of a stolen Huey gunship, the killers lure Ben into the trackless waste of the Arizona badlands. Reflexes dulled by years of wrong living, he is no match for the doomsday warriors. They want Ben to suffer slowly before he dies -- with no provisions, no weapons, no vehicle, no water.

No way.

RUN WITH THE DEVIL. Available wherever Bantam Falcon Books are sold.

AN262 -- 6/91

The Man of Bronze is back....

ESCAPE FROM LOKI
A DOC SAVAGE ADVENTURE
by
Philip José Farmer

For close to sixty years people the world over have been thrilled by the exploits of Doc Savage and his men. Now, for the first time since 1949, a completely new Doc Savage adventure has been written by acclaimed science fiction author and Savage authority, Philip José Farmer.

Every Savage fan knows that Doc met his men when they were all POWs in WWI, but the story of that first meeting has never been told in detail. ESCAPE FROM LOKI is the story of how 16-year-old Clark Savage, Jr. assembled the greatest team of adventurers and crime fighters the world has ever known.

ESCAPE FROM LOKI marks the beginning of an all-new series of DOC SAVAGE adventures. Available in June wherever Bantam Falcon Books are sold.

AN263 -- 6/91